Critical Praise for *River of Champions*

"A miraculous tale that shows the grit of ten boys
who banded together against all odds."
- Mike Nistler, *St. Cloud Times*

"If you like sports, you'll love this book.
If you like small-town stories, you'll love this book.
If you like an insight in what drives people, you'll love this book...
[it's] as much about people as it is about sports."
- Virg Foss, *Grand Forks Herald*

"River of Champions, a hockey must-read."
- *Minnesota Showcase Hockey*

"Very interesting reading, reflects the culture
and heritage of Minnesota."
- Herb Brooks,
U.S. Olympic Hockey Coach, 1980

"I kept thinking of *River of Champions...*"
Dylan Mills, Duluth East High School player,
speaking of the 1996 state tournament game
between Duluth and Apple Valley.
- *Minneapolis Star-Tribune*

"The images in the book are clear. The brutal cold
in the dead of winter in the upper reaches of Minnesota.
A sense of purpose. Unflagging teamwork."
- Sharon Raboin
Green Bay Press-Gazette

"Her book leaves a strong imprint,
a pure shot on goal."
- Bob Utecht, *Let's Play Hockey*

"...both inspiring and entertaining. Visualization is vivid: the pain, frustration of athletes and desire to take a stand and see it through to a championship conclusion."
- Tom Yelle, *Anoka County Union*

"Mary Schofield will take you back in those haunted northern ice arenas, those fragrant locker rooms, cold team buses and right to that remarkable '56 championship game."
- Don Boxmeyer, *St. Paul Pioneer Press*

"A story of Minnesota courage and determination... the team members face unbelievable odds, and their game will be etched forever in the history books."
- Paul Bergquist
Minnetonka Sun Current

"*River of Champions* inspires peewee team to explore state's hockey roots...does an admirable job of turning back the clock to the days of outdoor hockey."
- Rich Leonard, *Let's Play Hockey*

"If you like hockey, you'll love *River of Champions*."
- Steve Webb, *Rochester Post-Bulletin*

"...an interesting story, with fascinating details for anyone who's a hockey fan."
- Mike Fermoyle, *St. Paul Pioneer Press*

"...details the background of players and teams of that era..."
- John Gilbert & Roman Augustoviz
Minneapolis Star-Tribune

"Mary Schofield scored a hat trick. I felt on intimate terms with everyone on the team. It's a riveting story... a cross between 'Hoosiers' and 'Rocky'."
- Virg Foss, *Grand Forks Herald*

RIVER
OF
CHAMPIONS

To Jeff,

Thank you for scoring a hat trick for Christmas. This is a book my mother wrote — a true story, Northern Minnesota '50s. Enjoy! Merry Christmas to your whole family. EPC...

RIVER
OF CHAMPIONS

a novel
based on a true story

Mary Halverson Schofield

Snowshoe Press

This is a novel based on a true story.

For information, please address:

Mary Schofield
Snowshoe Press
P.O. Box 24334
Edina, MN 55424

Printed in the United States of America

First Printing: Four Directions Press .... Jan. 1995
First Snowshoe Press Printing .... Jan. 1999

Cover design by Mori Studio
Cover photograph by Mary Schofield: Andy Schofield #24 red

Pen & Ink Drawing by Glenda Gausen

Back Cover Photo - Left to Right
Front Row: Jimmy Reese, Jim Hall, Fred Dablow, Cal Offerdahl, Jackie Poole, Glen Carlson, Chip Strand.
Back Row: Greg Ranum, Art Cloutier, Duane Glass, Duane Erickson, Jon Wennberg, Dale Glass, Paul Bedard, Stanley Ranum.

edited by
Colleen Wasner
and David Starke

_____

*to my husband Darrell
and my son Andy
with love*

_____

Table of Contents

POSTLOGUE

AFTERWORD

Prologue

the town

It was cold in the town those years. The wind sucked in and belched down from the Canadian prairies. Minnesota stood defenseless before it as the line of demarcation between it and the arctic fell. Men retreated to their shelters, muttering; not blaming the gods, as men before them had, but certainly preferring the milder winters to the impositions of these.

Two hundred miles south of the town haughty farms yielded splendid crops on the rich, loamy soil, but here where the town was hostile earth glared up at the farmers and produced as little as possible for these stubborn men. One hundred miles east of the town men gouged into the earth, greedily extracting iron ores. Great forests were hacked down for more profit. From fortunes made by this plunder men were sustained in splendor. But where the town was, no minerals had been lodged in the earth. There was no forest stand. The few trees which determined themselves to grow were scrawny and thin-ringed. The barren land appeared levelly sandpapered from every direction.

* * *

Those years it was the winters that punctuated the town. The rivers crusted with thin ice that would crack at night with eerie booms. Unannounced blizzard clouds with heads raised in triumph screamed through the town spewing their white innards as they hissed, shrieked and bellowed. The sightless town waited. Then, when the storm was done, the moon would roll into the sky where the tormentors had been. Its paleness soothed the snow, joining moonbeams and snowflakes in an infinite peace. Or the snow would come in moist, thick flakes, lying down carefully without the wind -- or fine snow could swirl in playfully like a blissful child. Twenty above zero was warm in the winters of those years; the cold pressed down past forty below and, like an uninvited guest, became wearisome. Months of refrigeration preserved the snow. The town, a chameleon to the weather, would turn violet in the numbness. The sun, hanging suggestively in its southern arc, had lost its powers to warm. Then, like a long and painful labor, the winters would end with the wailing child of spring. Snows accumulated for many months meta-morphosed into water, and fled. The peaceful river enlarged, became frantic, roaring its new-found anger at its frothy swollen belly. The earth became oozy, sticky mud.

Then came the short coy summer bringing some peaceful days, pleasant in the idle sun. Other days brought clouds piling high and black that pounced on the town, obliterating it in water. Other times soft warm rains came to gently sprinkle the town and its gardens: a holy priest anointing hallowed ground.

For its enduring quality, the town was given a gift; a crown set upon its head by the gods of old. No crown of any royalty now or in ages past could match its brilliance. In the mid-1950s, great sunspots shot out from the sun's surface, creating dazzling auroras in the night sky. Neighbors would call to one another when the northern lights were dancing above them and the people would gather -- much as the Indians before them had -- to catch the spectacular show. From the peak of the sky, the lights tented down to the horizon, shimmering like a goddess spinning only in red, curtaining the night in giant streaks moving from apex to circumference. Or the lights would dance along the perimeters of the earth, unfurling green and white folding into one another in muted greens and bold whites. Or sometimes they would appear as opaque angels serene, hovering in peace safely above the battered earth; or, all three colors could emerge in a carnival atmosphere, dancing like mad demons against the black sky. Whatever the colors or the shape, they were grand and nothing, anywhere, could match their beauty.

The town had no college or industry. It had no wealth from past ventures. It possessed no historical importance and claimed no legendary heroes. It had no beautiful mansions or local battlefields. It did not even have a town square with a clocktower to grace it.

The town had far more than that.

The town had a spirit.

That spirit lived in a handful of unbridled boys as hope and pride and faith for the future and a determination that stubbornly refused to die. It lived in each of them, this spirit, and collectively this spirit had power. As conduits, these boys transferred the power to the people of the town, who lived through the boys and who cheered them on.

And right now that power belonged to the town.

Sometimes men accomplish
great things
miracles hanging on time
for the rest of us to remember
and sometimes
even on the brink of nowhere
in a white land
frozen and forgotten
boys accomplish great things

Mary Halverson Schofield

1

rivalry

"Hurry, Jackie!" Joey yelled crossly from the back porch door. He was used to yelling at his younger brother, who, in his estimation, rarely did anything right. There was no answer, but a telltale rustle from the kitchen reported that Jackie was putting his hockey jacket on.

"Let's go, we're late," he continued with a hurried voice to rush Jackie. Joey opened the door from the little unheated porch-like room, which buffered the kitchen from the outside, and felt the first whack of cold air.

Jackie trailed Joey to the chilly inside porch as he bit into a piece of sloppily jellied toast. With his other hand he tossed his hockey skates over his shoulder while simultaneously stepping into his black buckle boots. He patted his faithful black dog with his free hand as he was moving toward the door, and reached the door jam just as Joey let the porch door go. The door swung back hitting Jackie's toast hand, causing him to juggle his slice of breakfast. He almost lost the toast to his pooch, who wagged his tail furiously as he looked up eagerly. Jackie quickly shoved most of the toast into his mouth but gave his pet a piece as he shut the door carefully, leaving the dog in, and turned himself out into the cold dark morning.

Jackie took a deep breath of the frigid morning air. He hated those first stinging breaths of cold that made his gut ache and concurrently sent pain, like when eating ice cream too fast, throbbing through his forehead.

Joey's fluid athletic body was already running across the packed-down path in the snow to the garage as Jackie stepped out onto the small cement stoop at the rear of the house. He stopped to check the outside thermometer by the porch light. It was fourteen degrees below zero.

Clutching his hockey skates and stick to him, Jackie jumped off the little porch into the crusty snow to avoid the icy steps. He could hear the motor grind as Joey tried to start the car inside the unheated garage.

The invisible wind had worked itself up to a stinging frenzy against the cement gray of predawn, and the combination of wind and icy snow worked like a furious carpenter's sandpaper against

Jackie's face and neck. He wore his thick wool hockey jacket with soft golden leather sleeves, and was glad for the long underwear under his jeans. He pulled his stocking hat down over his ears and heard the car motor cranking as he sprinted for the garage.

Clouds hung low as the car made its way through the town's icy, deserted streets. It took the brothers only a few minutes to reach the banks of the desolate Thief River that wound through the town beneath the ice. Joey parked the car by a snowbank next to the bridge. They grabbed their hockey sticks and skates, jumped out of the car and sprinted quickly to the shore where other teenage boys were already lacing up their skates with numb fingers. It was too cold for conversation, but it was clear from their actions that these boys were there for a purpose.

* * *

Later, when the late-rising winter sun shone partially through the clouds, two huge high school boys, Jimmy and Cookie Reese, walking with the stealth and confidence of Siberian tigers, made their way across the snow-crusted bridge above the skaters.

Jimmy and Cookie, oblivious to the extreme cold and beating wind, were bare-headed and scantily clad for the severe weather. They wore jeans, open jackets with cotton shirts under them, and sneakers instead of boots. The younger brother, Jimmy, was lean and had craggy features. Cookie was slightly taller and bulkier. There was no expression on their toughened faces.

Midway across the bridge Jimmy and Cookie paused and watched the hockey players who were scrimmaging on the bumpy rink they had cleared for themselves on the thickly frozen river. Broken shovels stuck in snowbanks; two rickety nets sat in goal.

Jimmy and Cookie, hands jammed in their jacket pockets, watched silently until Jimmy wrapped his huge bare hands around the bridge's snowcapped railing and snarled in a bitter voice, "Dammit, Cookie, we should be on that team."

"Coach doesn't like us, remember?" Cookie answered hostilely, not taking his eyes off the boys.

Jimmy hunched over the railing, narrowed his eyes and growled, "They'd have a helluva lot better chance winning State with us."

As the brothers turned to leave, Jackie sighted them and waved his stick in greeting. Jimmy and Cookie nodded at him as they turned west, hunched their shoulders into the wind and continued their trek to school.

The sixteen river skaters were the Thief River Falls high school hockey team and were ranked number one in the state. Later that morning, as soon as the school pepfest for them was over, the team would board a school bus for the seven hour drive south to the state tournament. The contest would last for three days and the boys and their coach had every confidence that the state championship would be theirs.

The happy boys scrimmaged through the icy winds until Joey, their captain and undisputed team leader, called out, "We'd better get to school for our sendoff, guys!"

As the boys raced for shore Joey caught up with Jackie, scrutinized him for a minute and then said authoritatively, "You'd better behave at the pep rally, little brother."

Behind his black rimmed glasses Jackie glowered silently at his bossy older brother, who only gave him a second of a most superior and deflating glance before speeding off like lightning.

Anger propelled Jackie to shore. He was sick of being a little brother to a goodie-goodie. He was weary of Joey's put downs and he was tired of living in Joey's shadow. He knew he was as good a hockey player as Joey, but everyone only raved about Joey. He was Joey's younger brother, an afterthought in the hockey world, and he resented it.

Joey was going away to college next year. Then he, Jackie, could live his own life without a brother monitoring his every move and he could move into the spotlight and let the world know who he was. He would be the ace then.

It was a good thought but, unfortunately, not a very practical one because this year most of the good players would graduate and the players that were coming up were slim pickin's. The real question was, would there even be enough players for a team next year?

As a senior Joey was a shoe-in for the All State team but Jackie's chance of making it, as a junior, was only a distant hope. Next year looked bleak because in order to be considered for the All State team your team had to play in the state tournament. How would the Prowlers go to the tournament next year if they didn't have enough players for a team? Even if they did have a team how could they beat the other very strong teams in Region 8 to get to the tournament like they had this year? How could he ever settle his competitive score with his older brother?

The wind suddenly felt colder.

2

sendoff

Coach Rolle gathered his team around him for last minute instructions before they all stepped out of the crammed, stuffy stairwell at the far end of the gym that led up to the band loft one way and into the school gym the other. It was time for the Prowlers' sendoff to the state tournament. The band blared in the loft above them, muffling out the noise of the crowd.

"Just stay close together," Coach Rolle yelled above the band as he smiled at his team from under his fedora hat. "We'll walk out as soon as the band strikes up the school song."

Rolle was a young man in his mid-twenties, but to the boys he seemed middle-aged because he dressed in double-breasted gabardine suits and wore overcoats and brimmed hats, and because he was married and was part of the town's adult community.

Rolle beamed at his group of talented boys. "Follow me," he instructed them as he checked his bow tie and straightened his hat.

Rolle was a man with a powerful ego. He was also very intuitive, good looking, well organized, self assured and intelligent.

The band stopped and the noise of the crowd took up the background space for a few seconds. Then Doots Kellberg, the snazzy blonde drummer, rolled the drums and the school song started. The crashing volume startled Rolle and the boys.

> *"Cheer, cheer for old Lincoln High,*
> *Bear her standards ever on high..."*

The enthusiastic crowd sang. The gym was packed thick as bees and the doors were jammed with people trying to get in. Rolle gave the signal. The team, wearing their hockey jackets, quietly emerged from the door. The crowd cheered as the boys filed out. The band played with gusto from their cozy little loft above the basketball hoop.

Under the loft and above the basketball hoop was a huge, handmade, sagging banner that read "Go Prowlers 1955!"

The cheerleaders, wearing navy blue skirts and white sweaters, led the school song from the shiny wood floor.

*"...To her colors gold and blue,
We will always and ever be true..."*

The crowd sang vigorously.

The team followed Rolle, stopped when he did, then huddled close together like cows facing a wind and tried to assume comfortable stances for the occasion.

Rod Collins, the beloved and shy "Pooh Bear" goalie, shifted from foot to foot miserably, trying to look at ease. His arms dangled awkwardly at his sides like participles without sentences.

The fans sang on.

*"...In our hearts we ever will hold
Love framed in her blue and gold..."*

Chip Strand, a junior and Jackie's right winger on the second line, was comfortable with all of this hoopla and was all smiles. His warmth had won the hearts of the people who lived in the town. He glanced at Rod, who looked pale. "You alright, Roddy?" he asked.

"I guess so," Rod responded over the din. "I didn't expect this!"

"Great, isn't it?" Chip beamed back.

Rod didn't answer. There didn't seem to be any air left to breathe. Beads of sweat formed on his neck and ran down his back. He glanced at the others. They all looked hot.

*"...While her Prowler teams go marching
Onward to victory!"*

...sang the rollicking group. The school song over, the pleased-with-itself crowd took a collective deep breath and roared a mighty roar together.

Jackie looked like a caged animal out of its element but happy with the attention it was drawing.

Lone wolf defenseman Duane Glass, also a junior, postured himself to appear cool and relaxed, then locked himself in that position. He was a smooth, well dressed teenager, but also the toughest kid on the team and played that fact on and off the ice.

Junior Glen Carlson, Jackie's confident left winger, stood proud and tall. He was methodical to perfection in hockey and in life. He looked out across the crowd, mentally photographing the moment to savor later.

And Joey Poole, the hottest hockey player in the state and Mr. Popular of the school, looked like he'd come for his coronation.

Jimmy and Cookie sat stoically amid the wild crowd, elbows on knees, faces in cupped hands. Cookie grumbled to Jimmy without moving toward him, "Half of 'em are wimps. I hope they lose."

Jimmy, still looking forward, slitted his eyes and nodded icily.

Mr. Ostby, the principal, moved to the center of the gym and to the microphone set up for the ceremony.

Jackie looked around and noticed the attention was focused on Mr. Ostby. A devilish smile worked his face as he puckered up his lips and spit between his teeth, aiming at and hitting a freckled kid behind the ear. The kid, startled, looked around but poker-faced Jackie stared ahead innocently.

Joey glared at Jackie. A ripple of amusement ran through the group of players, but Joey was mortified. He should have stood closer to Jackie, but it was too late now.

Short, nervous Mr. Ostby with slicked back black hair, adjusted his glasses, raised his hand to quiet the crowd and spoke in a crisp, choppy voice, "We are all proud of the great hockey these boys have brought to Thief River!"

The crowd noisily clapped, hollered and whistled.

"We are proud that our school is representing Region 8."

The crowd hooted.

"We are proud to send these boys and their coach to the state tournament." He puffed out his chest and continued, "And now, here is Joey Poole! The Minneapolis papers say he is 'the darling of the ice' and the best skater in the state of Minnesota!"

Jackie rolled his eyes in disgust. This Joey thing was definitely getting out of hand.

The band broke into the pep song and the jovial crowd sang fervently as their beloved Joey headed for the microphone.

> *"P is for Prowlers pep*
> *R is for rah, rah, rah, rah*
> *O is for onward Prowlers*
> *W for winning way..."*

Tall and athletically built Fred Dablow and his best friend, Jim Hall, stood together like an American Gothic trying to blend into the gym floor. Being sophomores they certainly didn't want to call attention to themselves. Fred tilted his head to Duane on the other side of him, and said with a shaky voice, "You don't think we'll have to say anything do you, Duane?"

"I hope not. I do my talkin' on the ice," Duane drawled back.

*"...We'll take an L for Lincoln High,
E to elevate..."*

The crowd continued singing, not letting up its pace.

Jim nudged Fred with his elbow and warned, "Oh, no. Jackie's going to get that kid again."

The team watched wide eyed as Jackie spit on his innocent victim for the second time. The freckle-faced kid put his hand behind his ear, his eyes widening as he looked at the white stuff on his hand, then he looked back accusingly. Jackie had looked away. The boys on the team stifled laughter, except for Glen who was still scoping the crowd.

A softly beautiful high school girl was sitting in the bleachers with a girlfriend whom she nudged excitedly. "Glen Carlson just looked up here. Too bad he doesn't know I'm alive," she sighed. "He's so cute."

*"...R is for region champs,
So come on Prowlers,
Let's go on to State!"*

The crowd sang on and then roared and cheered at the finale.

On the floor a modest and blushing Joey took the mike. A winsome smile covered his face as he shuffled his feet and looked down at them. As the song ended the crowd broke into wild cheering. Joey looked up to the band loft at the stunningly beautiful clarinet player and homecoming queen, his girlfriend, Barbara, who smiled back at him.

As the din fizzled, Joey looked across the crowd, took a breath and said, "Thank you for the support you've given our team. I...the guys and I...all thank you." The band broke into "I Remember Only Joey."

Jackie grimaced.

Joey stepped back. Mr. Ostby smiled approvingly. The crowd roared again.

Mr. Ostby took the mike again and waited for the crowd to settle down, then said, "And now the coach of this fine team." He turned and looked back at Rolle and announced with great pride, "Dennis Rolle!"

Rolle strutted to the podium as if he owned it, and waved his hand gesturing "quiet" as perspiration oiled his forehead. He nodded at the principal, then with a beguiling smile scanned his audience. "Thank you, Mr. Ostby." He raised his voice a little, "I'm proud of this town," he raised his voice more, "and I'm proud of you fans...and..."

now Rolle was almost shouting, "I'm proud of this team!" The crowd cheered again. He put up his hand to calm the audience as his voice came back in quiet tones, "We will be over three hundred miles south of here in St. Paul. A lot of you will be with us, but to those who can't make the trip...our hearts will be with you!"

The cheerleaders waved their pom poms and jumped up and down, the crowd made a fierce racket and the peppy band played "When the Saints Go Marching In." The hot, noisy sendoff was over and it was time for the Prowler hockey team to board the school bus for the long trip south to St. Paul and the tournament games that would surely make them champions.

3

"whites"

Jackie laced his skates in the dimly lit locker room located in the basement of the St. Paul Auditorium. Their first game of the 1955 State Tournament was about to begin: the Thief River Falls Prowlers vs. the Minneapolis South Tigers.

Joey watched Jackie absentmindedly but critically from across the small, cramped chamber. It was a reflex action for him to watch his brother. He'd done it all his life.

Glen was dressed and ready. Everyone was talking just a little louder, he thought, and laughing a bit harder. Even the slamming of the locker doors clinked more sharply.

"We're finally here," Chip said as he grinned at Glen. Most of the boys had never been to Minnesota's Twin Cities of Minneapolis and St. Paul. Chip was one of them.

As juniors, Chip, Glen and Jackie formed the second line. They had played together, as a line, since they were Pee Wees. Seniors Joey and Sid Vraa, and sophomore Jim Hall, formed the first line. Duane Glass and Brad "Pud" Teale were the first line defensemen.

"Where's Rolle?" Jim Hall asked.

"I think he's at a coaches' meeting," Joey volunteered.

The team had bounced the many miles south on the stiff, cold school bus. It was below zero for the entire trip and not comfortable for anyone, except maybe the bus driver who had a space heater to keep him thawed.

Jackie's stomach felt knitted and beads of sweat were breaking out on his forehead and the game hadn't even started. He heard Glen saying something, probably to him, but he couldn't concentrate. He looked up to see Chip intently running his fingers along his rockered blades. It made his stomach feel better seeing this familiar, almost ritual, act of Chip's. He'd seen Chip do this ever since they were kids.

From across the locker room, Joey studied Jackie. All he could see was a mop of dark hair bent over the skates. Ever since they were little he always had to keep an eye on Jackie. Jackie was so unpredictable and wild. What would happen to Jackie next year when he, Joey, was away at college? Joey sighed. He had taken care of Jackie as long as he could remember, but none of his common sense seemed to rub off on his little brother. They were so different.

Joey knew what was right and he did it. Jackie just seemed to do what came into his head, without thinking. It was a mystery to Joey.

Chip and Rod were sitting together, ready to go on the ice. Rod was thinking about how the team got there...by winning every game and winning regionals. Now he felt frozen and detached. They were ranked number one in the state and for a moment he couldn't remember how to tend goal. Rod felt the panic rising. It started in his stomach and was creeping up inside him, slowly reaching his throat.

Chip sensed it and said without looking, "You'll be fine, Roddy...once we hit the ice."

Glen was talking to Jackie, but Jackie wasn't listening. That was unnerving. He needed to talk to Jackie. He looked around the dark, dumpy dressing room. Here they were at the huge St. Paul Auditorium, the Cadillac of Minnesota ice arenas, and the dressing room was small and cramped and smelly. The dressing room at home, in the little unheated Thief River arena, was big, clean and freshly painted, but here everything was dingy and dark. Something didn't feel right. Glen felt unsettled. Where was Rolle anyway?

Duane sat next to Jackie, but he was alone in his own world with his own thoughts. He was completely composed and ready to go, and just wanted the game to start. Duane was a brutal defenseman who knew what he had to do, and he was preparing to do it. No nonsense. He wondered where Rolle was. Game time was soon and Rolle was needed to get the team focused into one unit.

Jackie took a deep breath and tried to gather his thoughts. This first game they'd have to work hard, but they would win this one. Tomorrow a second game, and the next day the championship match and skating out under the lights. The guys had all wanted to skate under those lights since they were little. He couldn't think about that now. "One game at a time," Coach Rolle had said.

J.C., the volunteer assistant coach and history teacher, was setting out the old, worn, "dark" jerseys. Jackie liked him. J.C. understood the kids and Jackie appreciated his easy manner with them and his smirking eyes that matched his witty sense of humor. He cared about his students. Swede Lund, the assistant coach, wasn't with the team because the school couldn't afford to send him. J.C. paid his own expenses.

Right now J.C. felt a bit uneasy because Rolle wasn't there yet, but he didn't want to alarm the boys by looking at his watch. He knew it was getting close to game time.

Each team in the tournament was required to have "dark" and "white" jerseys, but Thief River came with only dark jerseys because that was all they had. The always-pinched-for-money school board couldn't afford two sets of jerseys. Rolle had requested the tournament officials that the Thief River team wear only dark and their opponents, who all had two sets of jerseys, wear their whites when they played Thief River. The fact that his school didn't have white jerseys was a major embarrassment to Rolle. His request was denied. Rolle had hoped to draw "dark" and avoid an unpleasant encounter altogether, but he had drawn "white" at the coaches' meeting that afternoon. Edina's coach, Ted Greer, offered Edina's whites but the officials would not allow a team that was in the tournament to lend jerseys to another team in the tournament. Rolle was out trying to round up white jerseys from a team not in the tournament.

Finally, a nervous Joey turned to J.C. and voiced what everyone else was thinking, "Shouldn't Rolle be here by now? It can't be more than ten minutes before the game."

Jackie heard that. It was the only thing he'd heard all evening and it rang through his ears and back out again. He was aware that Joey had been watching him earlier when he was lacing his skates. Joey always had an eye on him. Jackie thought about being alone next year and relished it.

"He'll miss our pregame talk," Rod added hoarsely. "He's never done that before. I need that talk." Rolle's talks quieted the boys down and revved them up at the same time.

Even Chip looked apprehensive and his ever-present smile was fading.

The others turned a worried look to J.C., who, trying to sound reassuring, said, "He should be here any minute now."

Rolle was aloof to the boys but, at the same time, had a quiet sense of humor that the boys appreciated. They respected him...and they all looked forward to his pregame talks. Where was their quiet, well-mannered coach who was always there for them? The air filled with uneasiness.

* * *

Next door, in the Minneapolis South locker room, the Tigers glued themselves to every word of their coach, Mr. Kogl. "We all know our opponents are favored to win this game and there's no question that Joey Poole is spectacular. Our game has got to be to wear Joey down. He's the fox and we're the hounds." He turned to his goalie, Roger Evenson, saying, "I have every confidence in you, Roger." The team nodded in unison, solemnly hanging onto and registering his every word.

* * *

Back in the coachless Prowler locker room the door suddenly banged open and bounced against the wall as a red faced Rolle stomped in. He spun around and beat his fists on the closest locker like a prize fighter hitting a speed bag, then jammed a fist between his teeth, still facing the locker.

The startled boys had never seen their even, composed coach lose his temper.

Rolle turned to J.C. and yelled, "They won't let us wear our dark jerseys!" Then he scowled at J.C., making sure this terrible information had registered with him. "Son of a bitch, what's wrong with these people?" His voice raised to a scream. The boys had also never heard him use that kind of language.

The team sat like wax dolls, not daring to move but trying to look at each other out of the corners of their eyes.

As Rolle ranted on, his fedora hat slipped to the side. "We'll be disqualified if we can't come up with white jerseys!"

The boys sat stock still, but inside each one of them this piece of news traveled like an electroshock treatment.

Joey opened his mouth to speak but like a jammed clutch, it stayed open but silent.

"Now surely, Dennis, there must be something we can do," J.C. spoke as calmly as he could.

Rolle was still screaming, "The officials will not let any other team in the tournament lend us jerseys! What's *wrong* with them?"

The boys sat as dark and unmoving as a highly trained Greek chorus.

Rolle looked at J.C., trying to gain a little control from his composed friend, but his face stayed beet red. "I called John Rossi, the hockey coach at Harding High School in St. Paul," he began. "We went to high school together in Eveleth. I wanted to borrow Harding's whites." He rambled hysterically, "I know he'd do it."

Jackie looked full at Chip, who was still sitting across from him. Chip was not smiling.

"Rossi wasn't home, but his wife said he'd call as soon as he got there. I've been waiting in the hotel room for two hours for a call back," Rolle ranted.

As he socked a fist into his open palm, Rolle talked to his hands,

"This snow held him up...but then he would have had to go to the school to get them and get all the way back here. He was coming to the game, of course..." his voice trailed off.

Rolle plunked down on a hard bench, moaning, "He could never make it now, he doesn't even know we need them."

A rap on the opening door was followed by a head peering around it. "Five minutes," the head tersely announced.

The locker room was as still as a fly in an icecube; the players as frozen and suffocated. No one could move, no one could breathe.

Jackie thought back on all the years of work that had gone into getting there. He was in a tailspin where he wasn't the pilot and a crash was coming over which he had no control.

The door cracked open behind Rolle. This time it wasn't the head, but instead, a stack of white jerseys that floated in with legs under them. The stack was thrown on a bench, revealing a smiling and friendly but obviously harried face.

"There a Rolle here?" the now full person asked.

"Yeah," a drained Rolle answered, looking at the white jerseys.

"Hi, I'm sorry to be late with these but the icy roads and jammed traffic were fierce out there. Rossi's wife called the school and asked me to bring these to you. I had to round up the principal to get his OK, so it's been quite a couple hours."

Rolle leaped up from the bench, grabbed the unsuspecting and welcome intruder, and gave him a bear hug. In a split second he was back to the affable Rolle everyone knew. "You just saved our hockey lives!" he bellowed, and then to the team, "Get the jerseys on boys and we're outta here!"

The suspended head appeared around the jarred-open door again. "One minute," it said.

Suddenly, everyone was alive. Jerseys hurled. "I can't find my number!" was being repeated by the boys. "Has anyone seen a seven?" Glen's nervous voice was stretched out and pinged like a taut rubber band. "I've got to have seven. There's got to be a seven somewhere," he wailed in desperation.

Rolle's voice boomed above the confusion. "Just get the jerseys on! It doesn't matter...just get something that will fit you." The frantic boys grabbed jerseys and pulled them hastily on over their shoulder pads. "It's bad luck not to wear our numbers," Glen moaned.

The other boys nodded sadly, as they looked at each other wearing the foreign whites. Rolle clapped his hands together with gusto, ignoring Glen's remark. "We're ready, let's go!" he said enthusiastically. Then he smiled benevolently and gently added, "Let's go get 'em."

David Reese, the student equipment manager who always had their equipment in perfect order, J.C. and Coach Rolle looked at each other with relief as their team filed out of the locker room. It had been a close call.

The mighty Prowlers from the north went out for their first game of the 1955 State High School Hockey Tournament wearing strange, white, city jerseys that read "St. Paul Harding Knights."

4

the game

The scene in the old, dark brick, solidly built St. Paul Auditorium was mayhem. Upbeat music that played loudly from giant speakers was overlaid by the sounds from the crowd. Fans sporadically cheered and then chit-chatted excitedly with their seat neighbors. Peanut vendors meandered through the aisles tossing bags, shouting, and being followed by people with crunched dollar bills in their hands.

From under the arena the Thief River Falls Prowlers readied to ascend the dark stairwell to the rink. Rod, as goalie, went first in the traditional lead, chewing his gum nervously. The fans, seeing the sticks of the players appear, began to roar for the team; the sound thundered down the stairwell.

Rod reached the top, saw the screaming mass of 7,500 people swimming before his eyes, and froze. The rest of the boys, walking hockey style, with eyes on the stairs instead of the players ahead of them, piled into Rod and each other, resulting in a domino, uphill traffic accident.

Rod clung to the railing at the top and just stared ahead, chewing his gum at the speed of light. "Je-sus Chr-ist," he gulped.

With a firm nudge from Chip, Rod moved out from the stairwell like a wound-down wind-up toy. The rest of the players sorted themselves out and waited patiently, except Jackie, who was near the end of the line.

"What's going on up there?" he yelled.

"Rod's a little nervous," Chip hollered back.

Rod had broken out in a cold sweat and was breathing in faint, nervy gasps. He clutched his hockey stick like an alcoholic clutching his gin, "Look at all those people, Chipper."

"Come on, Rod. We'll stay together."

A hefty guard opened the door and Rod stepped out onto the ice into the focus of the applauding, cheering crowd.

"You'll be fine," Chip said behind him.

Rod started skating, focusing on the newly made ice.

"Take deep breaths, Roddy. Take deep breaths," Chip coaxed.

The other players jumped onto the ice, looking up at the crowd as curiously as the crowd looked down at them. Joey immediately took off hot-rodding to the cheers and others followed suit, swatting Rod affectionately with their sticks as they went by him on the ice. Jackie looked a little impatiently at Rod, but swatted him anyway. He didn't care if the crowd was there or not. He came to play his game.

The Prowler cheerleaders ran out onto the ice with tennis shoes on. The girls, dressed in homemade blue corduroy slacks and warm white sweaters with TRF across them in blue and gold, began their cheers, yelling up to the rafters with enthusiasm and being answered by noisy, keyed-up fans.

Joey looked up to find Barbara. The tiny blue Thief River band looked like a small shiny blue button on a brightly colored bathrobe in the midst of the huge crowd. Joey couldn't see Barbara. Doots zealously rolled her drums as a signal to start the school song. The students sang lustily, but their effort was nearly lost as the Minneapolis South Tigers took the ice to a rallying roar from their fans.

In the radio announcer's box, Doug Teigmeier, the announcer from the Thief River Falls radio station, sat forward on his seat, arms crossed on the desk in front of a mike with the chrome letters, KTRF. A cup of coffee and a crumpled bag of peanuts were next to it. His voice boomed across the air waves, sending the game back home to Thief River.

He began, "This is radio station KTRF. Good evening fans! This is the game we've all been waiting for! Game three of the 1955 Minnesota State High School Hockey Tournament between the Thief River Falls Prowlers and the Minneapolis South Tigers. Excitement is high here tonight!" His delivery made the people of the far north feel rink-side.

* * *

At home in Thief River, Jimmy and Cookie made themselves comfortable in their dining room. Everyone who was home joined them as Cookie turned on the radio. Doug Teigmeier's voice boomed through static out of their large floor model wooden set.

* * *

Teigmeier paused and looked puzzled. "Something odd is happening, ladies and gentlemen. South High is out there but St. Paul Harding is the other team on the ice...no, this can't be. I see Joey Poole, racing around the arena like a streak. He's wearing a St. Paul Harding jersey!"

A man in a gray suit coat tapped on Teigmeier's shoulder and said something to him as Teigmeier held his hand over the mike. Animatedly, Teigmeier leaned toward the mike, "This is unbelievable! The Prowlers have borrowed St. Paul Harding's jerseys for the game! The numbers of the players are different..."

On the ice the Prowler team huddled around Rod, who looked like he was facing a firing squad.

"You OK, Rod?" Jackie asked apprehensively.

"Nervous as hell," Rod retorted.

Duane, cool and in charge, smacked Rod on the rear with his stick, "You'll be OK once we get started."

The buzzer sounded over Duane's last word and Joey broke out from the huddle yelling, "Let's go!"

period 1

Both teams scrambled for their places, either on the ice or in the box. As the boys got into position for the face off, the crowd noise reverberated from the rafters and Rolle yelled, "Let's go! Fire it up!"

Joey won the face off and passed the puck to Sid, who confidently lumbered down ice with it. Larry Alm, a defensemen from South who had the hardest shot on their team, zoomed in and stole the puck from the Prowlers when Sid passed it back to Joey. Alm, in turn, passed it to Bill Holm who passed it back to speedster Dale Rasmussen behind Rod's net, who snapped it back out to Alm. Alm had an awesome slapshot from the blue line.

Rod, mashing his chewing gum, got ready as the roar of the crowd rattled his ears. As soon as the puck was dropped, his panic had vanished. Now he was playing hockey. There was a friendly energy rolling around in the pit of his stomach that always came to games with him. He depended on that energy.

Alm passed the puck to Rasmussen, who headed down the ice toward Rod and his net. His eyes were concentrating on the puck and Rod was concentrating on Rasmussen and the puck. Rod bent his knees and held his stick parallel to the ice in front of him with one hand, while the other hand was out in front for balance.

"Get on him!" Rod screamed at his defensemen. "Take him out!"

Duane and Pud positioned themselves between Rasmussen and Rod's net as they drifted up on the intruder. Duane skated up on Rasmussen, rode Rasmussen near the boards, calculatingly braced his body, then smashed Rasmussen into the boards. A resounding slam echoed throughout the arena.

"Atta way, Duane!" Rod cheered.

The first period was brisk and tightly played by both teams. The Prowlers had breakaways and chances and shots on the South goal. Roger Evenson thwarted them all. Joey pulled out all his fanciest maneuvers, but the Tigers were on him and the openings he did find were adroitly closed by Evenson. Jackie pulled out his tricks. Nothing worked.

Joey was frustrated. Rolle was frustrated. Rolle took Jim Hall off Joey's line and put Jackie in wing instead.

"I think Jackie and Joey can get a goal together." He smiled at J.C., "We need to get on the scoreboard."

Joey passed the puck to Jackie at the face off. They played smoothly together and were both so fast that Rolle was confident they would get on the board.

But they didn't score either.

Near the end of the period there was another face off. Joey lost it. Hustler Jerry "Beaver" Westby picked it up and wound toward Rod, who drifted way out of the net yelling frantically to his defense, "Get on him! Pick it up!"

"Get back in the net!" Rolle screamed.

The fans picked up the chant, but Rod didn't hear it.

Joey caught up just as "Beaver" passed to Ekberg. Duane and Ekberg both flew at it. The puck got tied up in their skates and a face off was called. At the face off Koob, South's tall, lean center, jetted the puck to Rasmussen, who had moved into the slot. Rasmussen was on it and bing, bing, bing he ripped the puck to the inside pipe before Duane or Pud could defend it. It was so fast Rod's arm went up after the puck had hit the netting behind him.

Duane, poised and with sweat steaming off his body, swooped in as Rod dejectedly dug the puck out, "It's OK, Rod. It's our fault. No one was there to help."

Joey wasn't really worried. It was only one goal. He could match that.

In the background South fans yelled their heads off mechanically, "Ras! Ras!" while South's orange and black flew around the arena. Pom poms were up and toilet paper, tossed from under South's rafters, sailed around and around.

* * *

At home the Reese boys looked at each other.

* * *

period 2

Up in the announcer's box, the KTRF announcer, Teigmeier, adjusted his glasses, leaned forward, and fired away. "Thief River is behind going into the second period. Evenson is stopping everything the Prowlers are throwing at him!"

The first half of the period was scoreless. The Prowlers worked harder. Joey's line kept shooting. Jackie's kept shooting.

"Keep shooting!" Rolle kept saying. "One will get through eventually."

On the Prowler bench Rolle, bow tie crooked, hat askew, towel-rubbed Joey's head and talked intently to him, "They're all over you, Joey. Fake them out!"

Joey rushed onto the ice, as he always did, and picked up the puck. He danced by everyone as he skated toward Evenson with precision and charisma, working the fans like a pro. Sid and Jim flanked him. Joey stopped flat in front of a South defenseman, took two quick backward steps and shot. The puck bounced off Evenson's stick but Sid's stick was on it and, in a split second, he whacked the puck past Evenson and into the net.

The Prowler skaters dissolved into one lumpy hug and Rod waved his stick from the other end of the rink as delighted Prowler screams rose to the roof. Thief River toilet paper unraveled from the bird-watch rafters.

With the score 1-1, Joey's line skated off grinning triumphantly and Jackie's line skated on. Jackie saw that Glen was thinking and he knew that Glen was planning his exact moves if he got the puck. Chip acted impulsively; he wouldn't be thinking. Chip was speed on skates and a crash pilot with nerves tempered with steel.

Jackie, pumped up, snapped to them, "Let's get *our* act together and get one!" Jackie couldn't stand Joey's line being ahead of his in points.

Jackie won the face off and passed the puck to Glen, who skated it down and passed it back to Jackie. Norm Dahl zoomed in, intercepted the puck and sent it to his flank, who passed it to Ekberg. Glen had perceived the play and bolted for the puck, picking it off carefully. He had the net in his sights as he bore down on Evenson, faked out the defense and sent the puck through a knot of players and into South's net. Less than a minute had elapsed since Joey and Sid's goal.

Rod, alone on the far end, tossed his stick into the air. The crowd boomed, its echoes vibrating down to the rink. Again, the drums rolled and the small town band struck up, but was drowned out by the tumultuous throng. Glen's arms and stick flew in the air as he sailed around the goal to the waiting embrace of his teammates.

"We're on a roll now," Jackie predicted as they celebrated. "Let's keep 'em coming."

Doug Teigmeier practically stood as he leaned over the mike, hands pressed against the desk surface, "Carlson scores! Prowlers take the lead here in the second period!"

The game had started at 7:30 in the evening. The Roseau and St. Paul Johnson teams, who were playing the next game at 9:00, filed out of the arena, where they had been watching the game in progress, and into the dressing rooms. It was time for them to dress for their game.

Jackie got the puck. He skated deftly down ice and got past the defense. He felt wild and free on his one-on-one with Evenson. He would trick Evenson and Thief River would be two points ahead. Koob was a few strides behind Jackie. He knew it would be death to let Thief River score another. He pushed himself with all he had, caught up to Jackie from behind and, with his long arm, reached his stick out in front of Jackie and tripped him. Koob went to the box. Jackie swore under his breath.

* * *

period 3

The already thrill-a-minute game slipped into overdrive in the third period. Joey had performed like an arm of Mars, and Roger Evenson as sparing as the jackal at the door of Egypt's underworld.

Rolle pumped up the players on the ice, J.C. pumped them up in the box, and the players egged each other on, to push themselves to the limit.

The crowd never let up the insistent roar that rattled up the walls, through the helmets, and off the ice, bouncing back to the bleachers. The score was 2-1, the Prowlers holding the lead.

Rolle leaned over to J.C., "I'm going to have Joey float, and try for the quick break. We need another goal to protect our lead."

"That just might work, Dennis," J.C. answered as he intently watched the puck on the ice.

When Joey's line came off Rolle said, "Stand on the red line, Joey, and wait for a pass. Sid, get that puck to Joey." Both boys nodded. After the line change Rolle kept Joey's line on the ice longer than usual, hoping that Sid would get the puck to Joey and that Joey would get a breakaway and a quick goal. The South players practically stood on Joey. On the bench Glen leaned over to Jackie, "It's up to us. The entire team is locking Joey up." Jackie nodded, watching the ice.

At the line change Jackie was pumped up. He won the face off but lost the puck in a pass. As he turned quickly to get back into play he lifted his stick, trying to get it above his head on the tight turn. Instead, he whacked a South player in the chin. The whistles blew immediately and indignantly with the referees pointing at Jackie.

Jackie climbed into the box like a whipped lion into a cage. He wouldn't have taken a penalty now. Glen's heart was beating double time. He could feel it pounding through his ears.

Jackie sat in the penalty box and nervously watched the face off outside South's blue line. He could feel Joey's eyes drilling him for being so stupid as to pull a penalty and let the team down. And Joey was right. That was the thing of it, Joey was always right.

"They *have* to keep this lead," Rolle said to J.C. It was halfway through the period.

Glen won the face off and expertly passed the puck in Chip's direction. Rasmussen intercepted it and wound towards Rod. Duane braced and pressed the offender into the boards behind the net on the curve. Jerry Westby of South zoomed in the corner and whacked the puck out in front of the net. It hit the blade of a Prowler skate, deflected off, and tottered past Rod's goal line.

The goal judge, sitting on a high stool just off the ice, signaled a goal.

The South band picked up as the South fans yelled and waved their arms, "West-by! West-by! West-by!"

On the Prowler bench the team, Rolle and J.C. wore incredulous expressions on their faces. J.C. looked at Rolle and then back to the ice, "I don't believe it!"

"You've got to score," Rolle pleaded. "Get it in there!" he entreated them. Rolle pulled Duane and Pud out of defense and put Joey and Sid on the ice with Jackie's line.

That gave him four wings and one center on the ice. This strategy didn't work.

Rolle put Duane and Pud back on the ice playing defense and told everyone to play defense but Joey. He had to protect the match. Time was running out. The game was tied and nothing Rolle had tried worked. Evenson flopped on the disc, or he caught it, or he blocked it, or he got lucky and the puck hit the pipe.

The crowd, as was custom at the end of games, hollered with the clock, "Five, four, three, two..." counting down the end of the period and regulation play, "...one." The time had run out.

From the announcer's box Teigmeier, his voice betraying a surge of energy, shouted, "This hard-fought game is going into sudden death overtime!"

The Prowlers and the Tigers, sweaty and tired after giving the game all they had, sat on the roughed-up ice leaning against the boards, or sat on the boards, resting. The cheerleaders gave pep cheers in the background.

Chip, sitting by Rod, smiled at him, "You're doing great, Roddy." Rod masticated his gum and nodded stiffly.

Rolle went down the line saying over and over to the boys in the Harding whites, "Hang in there! You're out-shooting 'em!" or, "You're doing great," or, "Keep up the good work."

Duane and Pud had been formidable on defense. Only eight pucks had gotten by them in three periods of play.

South's last goal had been a fluke and Rolle was absolutely confident that his team would score quickly in the sudden death overtime. Evenson had had nineteen saves in regulation play.

Most of South's shots had been from out past the blue line because the Prowler defense kept the play away from their net. The Prowlers had been able to get in and pepper Evenson a few times and knew they could make that opportunity happen again.

Joey had no doubt that they would get one by Evenson quickly.

5

overtime

The Thief River fans, perched in their seats high above the ice, waited anxiously for the sudden death overtime. They missed the rollicking little rink at home, where they could lean over the boards and be part of the action.

"This is no good up here," Mrs. Strand, Chip's mother, complained to Mrs. Collins, Rod's mother, in her slightly Scandinavian accent. "I can't tell who Chipper is."

"I'm glad Rodney's in the nets so I can tell who he is real gut," Mrs. Collins answered in her Norwegian lilt. "But I miss seeing his face."

"They should score right off the bat," Mrs. Poole said to Cy Glass.

"Yes," Cy answered. "The Evenson boy has put on quite a show, but he's sure to be worn down by now. He can't last the pelting much longer."

The St. Paul Johnson and Roseau fans were eager for their teams to play the fourth tournament game, scheduled to start in fifteen minutes, after the Prowler-Tiger game. Their teams were dressed and sitting in stuffy locker rooms under the rink, ready to go out onto the ice for warmups.

The Prowlers were psyched up and eager to go after the short rest. The sudden death overtime would be five minutes, but no one expected it to last that long.

Rolle told his lines to keep shooting and Kogl told his to shut Joey down. Norm Dahl's assignment was to stick to Joey like glue, and South's defensemen were to shoot on Rod every chance they got. Pud and Duane had done a superb job of keeping the puck away from Rod's net.

Joey and his line started out on the ice to the renewed roar of the crowd, most of whom were standing. Joey planned a quick goal. "Let's try what we did before," he said to Sid as they skated out. "I'll shake Dahl. If I don't make the shot be ready for the rebound." Sid was always ready for the rebound, but he nodded like it was a new idea. They tried it, but Evenson wasn't to be had twice. His hand stopped the rebound as surely as a cat's paw stops a drugged mouse.

The Prowlers retried every trick they knew and Evenson stopped each and every one.

"What's wrong with us?" Chipper asked from the bench.

"I can't understand it," Glen answered him. "We've got to try harder."

Jackie's face muscles twitched as he watched Evenson stop another of Joey's shots.

The first five minute overtime ticked off scoreless.

During the five minute rest Rolle pumped them up and towel-rubbed their heads, giving each boy encouragement.

In the second sudden death overtime Joey was determined to put an end to the game. It was already time for the Roseau - St. Paul Johnson game to start. He saw the teams lined up outside the glass, waiting to get on the ice for their warm-ups.

Joey found a hole and darted through it; he was on a breakaway. Sid slid in and flanked him, ready for the rebound. The crowd was on its feet as Joey passed to him. Sid's muscular arms aimed the puck just above Evenson. Evenson was ready, too. Sid shot. Evenson's entire body pounced on it. The capacity crowd gasped.

Then Larry Alm got a shot and narrowly missed the corner of Rod's net. The fans "ahhhed" like a crowd watching fireworks.

Jim Westby, South's best stick handler and top scorer, wound around on a breakaway. Rod saw him coming. He had no help from Duane and Pud, who were behind the play. Rod bore down on his gum as Westby bore down on him. He had to make the save.

Rolle grasped the railing and gritted his teeth like he was on a roller coaster.

Westby let the puck fly and Rod blocked it.

Rolle gasped, "Whew." New beads of sweat stood out on his forehead.

The Thief River crowd was exuberant again.

Then Glen got a terrific shot off and Evenson made a terrific save, taking the shot with his left glove.

The second overtime period was scoreless.

* * *

Back around the big table with the Reese family, Cookie gloated, "They can't do it without us." But his face changed to a hint of sadness as he added, "I wish we was there to help the guys."

* * *

The Prowlers were getting tired. South wasn't falling for their routines and Evenson hadn't worn down. He seemed like a timeless demon put there to punish them.

The third overtime period included active shooting by both sides. In the last fifteen seconds Sid shot and hit the pole. The weary Thief River fans responded with a loud "ohhhhh."

The level of play flagged as the players' energy dropped.

The fourth overtime picked up with each team shooting on goal six times. It didn't help either team. The period remained scoreless.

* * *

The St. Paul Johnson and Roseau players retreated to their locker rooms, took off their skates and went back up to watch the game.

* * *

There was another five minute break. Everyone was getting edgy on the benches and in the crowd. Cokes and Hershey bars were passed out. Muscles were starting to ache.

The fifth five minute sudden death overtime was uneventful. Both teams ran out of steam. The Prowlers didn't get a shot on goal and the Tigers had only one from the blue line.

The boys drank, ate chocolate, rested and went back to the ice again.

Each overtime the boys had taken to the ice a little more slowly. The players, who had all worked to capacity, became more and more exhausted as the game wore on.

"What's wrong with us?" Chip asked in a wrung-out voice.

"We've got to come up with a goal," retorted Jackie, "...and *fast.*"

"No goal, no skating out under the lights," Glen warned.

"That can't happen," Chip groaned. "Our years of getting ready can't end now. This is what we've lived for our whole lives and now, when it's down to the wire, we can hardly skate!"

Their guts ached as they skated out for the sixth overtime. They played the five minutes skating and shooting and checking and stick handling as hard as they could but play sagged.

The teams sat on the ice again as their frantic coaches plied them with oranges and dextrose pills.

The seventh overtime dragged on with no end to the contest. The Tigers got five long shots on Rod.

The crowd was exhausted. They had screamed until their voices gave out, then the cheering decreased to a moaning that merely rose and fell. The impatient Johnson fans started yelling, "We want

Johnson! We want Johnson!" as the drained Prowlers and Tigers sat for their five minute rest.

* * *

The boys from St. Paul Johnson and Roseau retreated to their locker rooms to put their skates on again and somehow the St. Paul Johnson locker room door got locked from the outside. After much pounding by Johnson, someone from Roseau heard them and went to find a janitor to let them out.

* * *

On the ice the play went into the eighth overtime. Both teams were emotionally and physically kaput. They couldn't get a full breath and their legs didn't want to move as they struggled to get the elusive goal.

Teigmeier caught his breath after a commercial, "Ladies and gentlemen, history is being made here. I have just been handed a memo that the record number of overtimes ever played in the state tournament was four, *until tonight!*"

As the boys rested after the eighth overtime, their concerned parents watched them sprawled out on the ice. Some players actually dozed off.

"I never heard of such a thing," Mrs. Strand complained to Rod's mother. She was small and wiry, but had a voice that carried.

"It's a wild one alright," Elmer Poole answered back.

"Those boys look so darn tired," Mrs. Strand continued. "I think they should get some sleep and then come back tomorrow."

All the parents nodded in agreement.

"The officials will stick to the rules and the rules say the game will be completed," Paul Bedard, the coach of the Thief River semi-pro hockey team, put in softly.

"Well, those officials should use some sense," Mrs. Strand retorted, and everyone knew she was right.

The ninth overtime droned on. Shots on goal were in slow motion and saves were the same.

Finally, when players and watchers could take no more, a voice boomed over the loudspeaker, "The first period of the next game of the night will be played. We will resume this game during the first period break of the St. Paul Johnson - Roseau game."

"Well, thank heaven's for that," Mrs. Strand lilted.

The depleted, exhausted, worn-out boys from South and Thief River skated off the ice for a rest in the locker rooms. The fans sighed a sigh of joint relief.

As the teams dragged themselves off the ice, the Roseau and St. Paul Johnson teams skated by, refreshed and raring to go. They had waited, dressed in full equipment, over two hours to play their game. A St. Paul Johnson senior, Herbie Brooks, skated by nodding at Joey and kiddingly grumbled at him for taking up their ice time.

Glen, leaning on his stick for support, glided slowly next to Chip, letting the ice do the work. "How can they skate so fast?"

Chipper looked at the boys and answered miserably, "My legs are rubber."

Jackie, bent over from the waist and holding his stick across his knees, chipped in, "You're lucky, mine are wood."

Joey, dragging behind, complained, "I can't even feel mine!"

"At least you can see," Rod added. "The ice keeps moving like a huge wave in front of my eyes."

J.C. and Rolle looked at each other as they walked behind the boys. J.C. edged a little closer to Rolle, "It seems as if this game should be played in the morning." Rolle nodded a tired nod, "Kogl and I already asked. The officials won't do it. We've got to keep them going as best we can."

The team piled into the uninviting locker room and collapsed onto the solid wooden benches as the Roseau - St. Paul Johnson game started. It was 11:33. Piles of oranges, little wooden crates of Cokes in small bottles, and boxes of Hershey bars lined the room. Rolle and J.C. passed out the rations and tried to keep the conversation light.

"What are you trying to do out there?" Rolle joked. "We're supposed to win a hockey game, not skate an all-night marathon!"

The pie-eyed boys, like thrown-out mannequins, sat staring blankly.

The tenth five-minute sudden death overtime, starting after midnight, dragged to an uneventful conclusion. Half-hearted shots and half-hearted saves. Underwater illusions.

Again the announcer's voice: "We will resume the Roseau - St. Paul Johnson game's second period. This game will continue between the second and third periods of that game."

Now all touch with reality had left. The boys were shadows moving off the ice. They sat in the locker room unfeeling, untalking, undone. They drank Cokes and forced down some more chocolate, while some snoozed on the benches and the floor and then, with aching legs, they tromped back up the stairs when Rolle told them to.

They skated onto the ice to weary cheers to play another sudden death overtime. Through the looking glass, down the rabbit hole.

Teigmeier, weary and bleary-eyed in the announcer's box, nodded a thank you to a woman handing him a cup of coffee and continued with a slight rasp. He ran some fingers through his hair and intoned feverishly, "This is unbelievable! We are going into *eleven* overtimes of play here tonight. It's 12:20 a.m!"

* * *

Jimmy took a last gulp of Coke as he and Cookie sat at the table alone now. All of their brothers and sisters had gone to bed. They didn't talk, they just sat and listened to Teigmeier.

* * *

In the eleventh overtime, a comatose Duane and a pooped-out South player collided sluggishly into each other about five feet from the boards. The referee's whistle blew. The referee skated over and signaled a penalty to Duane.

Joey stood ashen, feeling a chill creep up his spine. This penalty wasn't right.

Duane, a surge of wakefulness rushing to him from angry disbelief, demanded, "What was I called for?" The paunchy referee snarled, "Boarding!"

Gut rage poured itself into Duane, and he felt his tired knees quaking with it. He felt his heart pumping with it. He felt his face reddening with it. The kind of rage anyone would feel being unjustly accused. He wouldn't have had the energy to board anyone even if he wanted to. He felt like punching the referee square in his nitty jaw, but he was too tired. He looked imploringly to Rolle.

All that was going on with Duane took just seconds. Simultaneously from the Thief River bench, beet-faced Rolle screamed "*No!*" The Thief River crowd dissolved into a sound wave of hissing and booing.

South's fans sat quiet.

Over the loudspeaker, the house announcer was heard, "Penalty on Thief River Falls, No. 9, Duane Glass. Boarding."

Everything hushed as a seething Duane headed for the penalty box. He got in, sat down on the bench, slammed down his stick and pressed his forehead onto the railing. His stomach was racing but his brain was numb.

In the stands Duane's outraged father exploded, "What a time to call a cheap penalty!" Heated up, he continued, "Can you believe that call?" He was all but pacing in front of his narrow seat. At the same time he had a sick feeling in the pit of his stomach.

The Thief River fans were furious. It was clear to them that the referees wanted the game over, and it was also clear to them who the referees wanted to win.

Rolle, faced with the bad break, put Jackie on Joey's line with Joey and Sid. Joey got the puck and skated down the ice slowly, his gravelly voice yelling frantically, "Come on, Jackie!"

Jackie, too tired to have his usual thoughts about his brother being bossy, tried. God, but he tried. He started skating down ice. Joey weakly passed the puck to him. Jackie exerted all the energy he had but all that happened was that his knees buckled under him like a cheap assembly-line gadget, and he landed flat on his face.

Agonizingly slowly, a South player got the puck and, as if he were skating in cold syrup, started painfully up the ice with it. Joey mustered every ounce of energy he had left and tried to thwart the player. The player's sore arms shoved the puck towards South's Jim Westby as he fell, sending his energy with the puck. Pud got a piece of the puck but couldn't control it. The puck ended up in front of Westby, who, wanting a line change, mustered up his strength and slapped the puck towards the net from the blue line. The arena became stark quiet.

Joey saw it, but he was too far back to do anything about it. Jackie saw it from his prone position on the ice. Glen and Chip saw it from the bench. Rolle saw it and looked anxiously at Rod. The puck sailed low like a bat toward the net. Coach Kogl stood perfectly still. Those in the crowd who weren't already standing rose slowly to their feet. Two players screened the shot and Rod didn't see it as it sailed by them and him into the net.

In the announcer's booth Doug Teigmeier's sad voice tunneled, "Minneapolis South has won the game."

6

aftermath

It was dark in the room Jackie and Glen shared at the St. Paul Hotel, except for a light filtering in the window from the marquee outside. The cathedral clock chimed three doleful gongs. Jackie rolled over.

Glen's voice, soft from defeat, questioned, "You awake, Jackie?"

There was a slight pause, then a sigh from the other bed, "Yeah."

Glen snapped on the lamp that was between the beds. He was wearing neatly pressed pajamas. Jackie was clad in rumpled shorts with no shirt on. Their faces were tear-stained. Glen laid back down like an old lady lays out her pearls, carefully, so as not to hurt his strained and weary body.

Jackie sat up and propped the pillows behind him, "I wonder if the picture will ever go away."

Glen responded, detached from the question, "What picture?"

Jackie stared beyond nowhere. His voice cracked, "The puck going past Rod."

Tears streamed down Glen's face, "Probably not."

Jackie dug under the mattress for a pack of cigarettes and lit one up.

Glen noted dully, "You shouldn't do that here. You might get caught."

Jackie ignored him and took a long and satisfying drag on his cigarette.

Glen forgot his remark as his face took on a different look. The pain was there but super-imposed over it was an added look, a cross between stubborn and defiant. His tone rose as he spurted, "We've got to win next year. It's our last chance."

Cigarette caught in his teeth, Jackie angrily punched the firm mattress, then exploded, "Damn! We should have had them *tonight*." He inhaled hastily and stared down the wall. Glen refluffed his pillow and rolled over onto his side, reciting matter-of-factly, "We weren't tough enough."

Jackie took another drag off his cigarette and squinted his eyes, headache style, still fixing them on the wall. "Duane's tough." He paused for a second and then continued, "We've all got to be as tough as Duane."

Glen got out of bed and walked toward the window. He parted the heavy floor-length curtains and gazed outside into the night. "There are only seven of us left," he lamented. His eyes moistened as he quietly continued, "We can't win with seven." He turned an over-stuffed chair around to face the window, plopped down in it and looked out. Jackie flicked his cigarette.

After awhile Glen wistfully remarked, "If Jimmy and Cookie were on the team..." Outside the window plump snowflakes hovered ever so slightly before reaching the ground. Jackie agreed, "Now you're talkin' tough."

Glen sighted the cathedral tower as his voice intoned to himself, Jackie and the universe beyond, "God, I hate to lose."

beginnings

Jackie snuffed out his cigarette and let his body go limp onto the crispy hotel sheets. Glen sat in the overstuffed chair looking out over the sleeping city. They drifted alone with their thoughts back to another world. It was the world they shared as children.

Bud and Bob

"Glen, Chip, hurry!" a little Jackie yelled in brimming excitement. "They're out there!" Little tufts of dark, curly hair jutted out from his stocking cap as he jumped up and down on the crunching snow.

Glen and Chip ran toward Jackie, their little skates clinking. "We're coming! Wait up!" The southern winter sun beat down on them but gave little warmth as they ran knee high through the fresh, powdery snow.

The boys joined and ran hastily down the block to the hockey rink by the Lutheran Church. The other boys were already there and motioning frantically for them to hurry.

There, on that rink, Bob Baker and Bud Brussoit of the town's semi-pro team the Thieves, were doing one-on-ones, ripping up the ice with sensational stick handling and body moves. The little boys hung over the boards that lined the rink, yelling and whooping at the exhilarating command performance witnessed only by them.

A hockey puck rested on the ice. In a flash a hockey stick was on it like a snake zapping an unsuspecting mouse. On the other end of the stick was Bud Brussoit, grinning like Kipling's snake, Kaa. He dashed off with his prize, his skates briskly scraping the outdoor ice. His jacket flapped in the wind but a tight blue stocking hat, the squat kind, kept his hair in place. He was short, stocky and cunning. He pulled his brows unconsciously toward each other and dodged past the other skater on the rink, Bob Baker.

Bob, tall and graceful, stretched out his limber body, extended his arm and curled his stick in front of Bud. Bud listed to the outside but Bob quickened his pursuit and his skates appeared to be running across the ice. As he caught up to Bud, Bud stopped abruptly, snow flying, did a pirouette and came out aiming for the net and shot all in one move. Bob dove in front of the puck.

The skaters were eighteen, the town hot-shot hockey players. Back and forth they sparred, from one end of the boarded hockey rink to the other, oblivious to anyone or anything but their play. The show dazzled. The little boys were the only spectators.

The boys hung over the boards, arms dangling, watching wide-eyed the supreme performance of their stars. Glen, knitted cap pulled right down to his eyebrows, talked to Jackie at his side while his head turned back and forth, following the direction of the players.

"Baker's the greatest hockey player in the world," he breathed. "I'm going to be like him someday..." Glen paused as Baker whizzed past leaving a breeze behind, and then finished, "...smooth." He looked briefly at Jackie with conviction.

On the rink, the awesome ice gods performed. Sometimes they spun and charged down ice so fast they became blurry images. Sometimes the sunlight caught on their skate blades and they looked like they were skating on diamonds, or just light.

Jackie banged on the boards, blinking in the sun through his black-rimmed glasses, and talked tough to Glen, "I'm gonna be like Brussoit." His eyes sparkled as he made a meaningful pause, "Tricky."

Chip stood straight up, clapped his hands to the boards and looked to either side of himself, talking to everyone, "Let's hurry and get out there or we won't be like anybody!" Bud Brussoit stormed by, winking at the boys. Jackie cupped his hands around his mouth and yelled down ice at him pleading, "Will you guys skate with us?"

Bud made a clean wide circle and shouted back, "Sure, if you hurry!"

The boys gave war whoops and scrambled to the warming house to put their skates on, like fleas before the dip.

up the river

Glen and Chip were alone, lacing their skates on a log next to the river. The hard wind had swept the ice clean of snow. Huge cracks lined the river, but the ice was many feet thick and the cracks were frozen over on another, deeper layer. It was still and cold. The sky was a violet, velvet cape covering them.

The boys finished the lacing, blew warm breath on their stiff hands, grabbed their mittens and jumped out onto the densely frozen river. Glen dug a puck out of his jacket pocket and dropped it onto the ice, casually passing it to Chip, "We'll have to be careful not to lose it in the snow. We can't miss the passes," he said somberly. "It's the only one I have."

Chip covered the puck with his beat up stick blade and twirled around with it, "Chipper the Great never misses!"

The two little skaters started down river. They were alone on the ice sheet that stretched large and silently before them and the sky was so blinding white they couldn't tell where the river banks ended and the prairie beyond started.

They skated for a long, long way never seeing anyone, or any animal or any bird, passing the puck and jumping the cracks as wide as yardsticks, flipping the puck over them. They skated wild and free as well-fed wolves who sensed their territory was safe and took their time to play. Then they stopped, huffing and puffing to catch their breaths. The sun had sunk low to the south.

"How far you think we've come, Glen?"

Glen's eyes shone bright from his pink face, "I don't know. It's farther than we've ever been before."

"We'd better start back, sun's getting low." Glen pocketed the puck and the boys, alone in their world, raced back toward the sinking sun, jumping the cracks and laughing as they went. The innocence of childhood followed them as the ridge of the sun exited the earth.

under the lights

There were no more snowfalls and the temperature stayed under twenty below, which kept the river skating perfect and the boys took advantage of the good ice. One day, after skating since sunup, they took a lunch break. Duane, Glen, Fred and Jim roasted hot dogs and potatoes in a campfire they had built, while the other boys munched down sandwiches as they sat on logs. They ate with their skates still on, their hockey sticks strewn on the ground. The bright sun hung in a low arc at the southern horizon. The snow sparkled.

Jackie bit into a sandwich and talked with his mouth full, "What can be better'n this? Two days to skate all day." He swallowed and took another chomp, "I hate school!" Chip stood up from his log and pointed to the river. "Look! There they are!"

Flying across the ice were players from the town's semi-pro hockey team. The boys watched them intently. Joey, absently holding a sandwich, looked hypnotized. "I'm going to skate like that someday," he said with conviction.

As the skaters sailed around the bend Duane practically shouted, "Baker's trying out for the Olympics in Czechoslovakia!"

Jackie answered, but his eyes were still on the skaters, "He'll make it for sure," he said as the last skater circled the bend and disappeared.

The boys relaxed back to their lunches. "You know what I heard?" Chip's eyes flashed with excitement as he relished what he was going to reveal to his friends. "I heard that at the state high school hockey championship game they turn off all the lights and then they announce each player."

Jackie pulled a candy bar out of his pocket, unwrapping it quickly.

Chip continued, "And then each player gets to skate out under a spotlight!" Chip nearly swooned over this.

"Oh, wow," Glen answered back, running his hand across a blade of his skate to remove the snow.

"I want to do that someday." Chip talked in a hushed, faraway voice.

Glen added dreamily, "Me too."

Jackie bit into a chunk of his candy bar and, mouth chock full of caramel, peanuts and chocolate, matter of factly spoke out, "I just want to play there...and win."

Duane stretched and then leaned over, retrieving his hockey stick. "What are we wastin' time for? Let's play hockey!"

The boys hastily stuffed the last chunks of food in their mouths while jumping down the bank onto a homemade rink on the river. While they began to warm up again, two huge-for-their-age boys skated up. They were Jimmy and Cookie, the standoffish brothers from the other side of town. Cookie was smoking a cigarette.

"Where'd you get that?" Jackie asked, impressed.

Cookie swaggered his answer, "Bernerd."

Glen stared in disbelief, "Your brother? He gave it to you?"

Jimmy, unimpressed with the conversation, replied, "You kiddin'? He swiped it outta his jacket."

Jackie looked at the cigarette and asked Cookie, "Can I try it?"

Cookie handed it over, "Sure." Jackie took a long puff and acted tough, right before Joey skated over.

"Jackie! Stop that, I'll tell Mom!"

Coming around the bend, in flowing black robes and looking from the distance like a raven skimming the earth, skated Father Noah, the local Catholic priest. He carried a hockey stick and waved it as he headed towards the boys.

Joey happily waved and called out, "Father Noah!"

Jackie turned white, his eyes popped open. He coughed out the cigarette and covered it with his skate blade while Cookie mumbled "Shit" under his breath.

In skated the smiling Father Noah. Joey looked up at him admiringly, "Will you play hockey with us, Father Noah?"

The priest looked down and winked, "I was hoping you'd play hockey with me!" The kind priest's eyes twinkled.

Other boys were skating in for the pick up scrimmage that took place every Saturday afternoon on the river. Everyone was welcome and everyone played. Sides were picked quickly and the scrimmage was on.

Jackie and Joey faced off. Joey got the puck and passed to Jimmy who passed to Fred. Cookie came barreling in and knocked him down. Father Noah, his dark robe sweeping the ice, got the puck and passed it to Art, who lunged for it and fell. Chip picked it up, swirled around the goal, accelerated down ice and passed to Jimmy. Jackie intercepted it, sped down ice and shot at Cal Offerdahl, who stopped the puck easily.

Father Noah shouted over to Jackie, "Jackie! Come here!"

Jackie skated over to the crusty, sincere priest who affectionately grabbed Jackie by the hair on the back of his head. "Wanna be a good player?" Father Noah asked. Jackie nodded.

Father Noah squatted to Jackie's level to talk eye to eye. "Discipline yourself. Learn to pull the goalie out and learn teamwork. It will be worth it."

Jackie skated back to the others, soaking in the advice and pleased that Father Noah told him this and not Joey. Joey was bossy and Joey knew everything.

Thieves

An old light dangled in the rear of the building. Ice shavings were piled ten feet high on both sides of the door. Jackie, Jimmy and Cookie passed a shared cigarette around in a clandestine manner. Glen and smiling Chip, always in the right lane, came up. Glen looked at them alarmingly; Cookie looked back at him disdainfully.

"Hey, you guys better stop that. You'll get in trouble if you get caught," Glen warned.

"We won't get caught," Jackie retorted in a superior manner. The boys finished the cigarette and all of them crawled through a window situated near the ground. The boys popped out from behind shovels that were stacked in front of the low window and moved to the first row where they cut in next to Jim, Fred, Art, and Duane. They all hung over the boards, pounding them as the semi-pro players, wearing jerseys that read "THIEVES", swooshed by, warming up.

Except for the polished Bob Baker, the Thieves team was wild and woolly.

A boisterous male crowd lined the dingy arena. All stood. There were no seats. There was no heat.

"Greek" Swanson skated to the Thieves' net; Bob Baker took the face off that he won. He passed the puck to Morris "Mouse" Efdeland who skated down ice and passed the puck to the other wing, Bud Brussoit. The crowd hollered. A huge burly defenseman with no upper teeth between his canines tripped Bud. A nasty fight ensued.

The little boys yelled, "Get 'em Bud!"

The referees managed to separate the offenders and dragged them, still snarling, off to the penalty box.

The game went on with the boys cheering every move. This was their winter entertainment. They never tired of playing hockey themselves or watching their idols play.

The center from the other team had the puck and passed it to his wing. A large and overpowering Thieves defenseman, Tony Dorn, riding backwards on his skates, squared his shoulders for a hit. The wing turned on speed to get past Dorn who turned on his own speed and slammed the wing into the boards by the boys.

Duane grinned, "Atta way Dorn!" Then he drawled to Jackie, "I wish we had a team for us. I wanna do that."

Bob swooped in, stole the puck and skated up ice flanked by Bud. The crowd roared. He pulled his stick back and aimed. The goalie readied. Bob faked the shot but at the last instant and without looking at him, flicked the puck to Bud who caught it on his stick and drilled it behind the goalie, into the net.

The boys stood like small, wide-eyed statues for the split second it took for this move to set in. Then like little Roman candles they screamed and danced up and down.

Jackie yelled above the madhouse, "Did you see that? *Did you see that?*"

Glen shouted back, "He didn't even look at Bud!"

Chipper, still in a state of shock, screamed, "How did he know he was there?" The boys became quiet amid the throng.

Glen, his doleful eyes serious, quietly asked, "Can we ever be like that?"

Jackie looked at him bold-faced and without hesitation, "You bet your ass we can!"

8

team

Jim and Freddy, now thirteen, ran along Main Street towards the river, intent on where they were going. They were clean cut American-boy-athlete types. Their sticks were slung over their shoulders with their skates tied to them. There wasn't much snow yet, just some teasy white stuff that encircled their feet like dried cotton candy. It was mild November cold; the intense cold of winter had not yet set in.

They reached the part of the river where the bank was built up to accommodate the bridge, jumped down the bank "crosscut" style, as if they had skis on, and yelled excitedly, "Guess what? Guess what?"

The other boys were already skating on their river rink. Glen and Chip were fixing up a goal which was made of logs and sticks. All the boys looked up curiously.

As Fred reached the river's edge he megaphoned his hands and bellowed, "There's going to be a team!"

"A *real* team!" Jim shouted. "A real team for our age!"

Jim and Freddy raced onto the ice and the skaters drifted towards them questioningly.

"The new Thieves coach from Canada is going to coach us! His name is Paul Bedard!" Freddy announced. Freddy and Jim were all but dancing on the clear ice.

The boys looked at Jim and Freddy like they'd announced the Second Coming. Jackie threw his stick in the air, howling, "Hot damn! All our skating is finally going to pay off!"

* * *

Posters with information about the team went up around the little town and every boy Pee Wee age with skates answered the call for tryouts. Joey, a year older than Jackie, and Cookie, a year older than Jimmy, were too old for the team.

The big day came. Inside the unheated, drafty Thief River Falls ice arena, a tin quonset affair of boards, ice and hay, the boys anxiously tied up their skates.

Coach Bedard, a kind, wiry man in his twenties, pulled on a shirt that said, "THIEVES".

Jackie leaned over and whispered to Glen and Chipper, "Let's

listen to everything he says so that we can practice it on the river."
They nodded solemnly.

Chip added, "With our skating and his coaching we can skate out
under those lights someday."

Jackie reached for his stick and replied boastfully, "I know so,
Chip. We'll put this town on the map."

Bedard got up from the bench casually, smiling warmly, "All right
boys, let's see what we can do, eh?"

The boys sprang out onto the ice with so much vigor, it startled
Bedard and he chuckled as he followed them. "All right boys, let's
learn what drills are."

The bright and enthusiastic new students learned a circle drill,
then to skate from end boards to the red line and back and then to
the blue line and back as fast as they could. Bedard blew his whistle
and led them into passing drills, up and down the ice. Like ducklings,
they followed his every move, recording each for future use. They did
three-on-twos. Jackie skated down ice with the puck and made a
goal. Bedard blew the whistle, "Boys, boys, stays on your wings. Do it
again!" The boys repeated and repeated until they got it right.

Paul Bedard selected his team. As a coach he watched them, he
taught them. He was patient while they learned, he was tough in
what he expected of them. He got them jerseys and other teams to
play against and made them into a real team. He was their first
coach, as good as a coach could get, and they never forgot him for it.

The season was a smashing success. They beat every team they
played and Bedard entered them into the state tournament, put on by
the American Legion, in Eveleth. He knew they had a lot to learn by
playing tougher teams and he knew Minnesota's iron range towns
had them.

The day before the team left for Eveleth the boys sat in the old
brown booth at the back of the Rexall drug store. They had grown
cocky from their successes over the winter and were at the point of
being boisterous.

"Eveleth better move over," Duane bragged, "Thief River's comin'."
He gulped his green river.

"Can there be anyone better'n us out there?" Chip questioned.

Jackie blew the outside wrapper of his straw past the booth and
sat back, "I don't see how. We've beaten everyone for miles around."

9

eveleth

The Eveleth Hippodrome was a real building with an ice skating rink in its belly. It was not like the makeshift affairs the Thief River Falls Pee Wees were used to skating in. It was built of bricks and had rows of seats and the seats were filled with people.

The boys huddled around Bedard, raring to go. A cheer went up as the "home" Eveleth team skated out. The Thief River Pee Wees turned to watch and got quite a shock. Huge, self-assured, magnificent skaters circled the ice in a tightening coil. Team ace, Jerry Norman, was six feet tall and had a moustache. The entire team was big, formidable, rough, aggressive, and talented. The Thief River boys paled in comparison.

As the Eveleth team warmed up, pro style, on their half of the ice, the Thief River team stood at the blue line watching them in panic.

"That Norman kid's bigger than my dad!" Jackie blurted uneasily.

Glen pulled himself together and answered toughly, "We'll just have to outskate them."

Jerry Norman, Don Judnick and Jimmy Rossi, all huge boys, tore out from near the net on some self-imposed drill. Charging for the forlorn little group standing at center ice, they stopped on dimes. Ice sprayed like snow through a snowblower covering the crestfallen group. Smiling like cats squashing mice, the Eveleth boys darted back to their team.

"So much for outskating them," Chip moaned.

Duane clenched his teeth and muttered, "I don't have a good feeling about this."

A whistle signaled the beginning of the melee. Jackie felt the sweat on his neck as he faced Jerry Norman. He tried not to think about the giant gloating above him and concentrated, instead, on the puck. The referee dropped it and Jackie, who was closer to the ice than Norman, won the face off and zipped it to Chip. Jackie dropped back, ready for Chip to pass it back to him. The plan was interrupted when Drobnick flattened Chip. Jerry Norman picked up the idle puck, flashed by Fred and Duane like a rocket through clouds, shot and scored.

"Atta way, Jerry!" Drobnick yelled to his friend as the crowd cheered.

* * *

Glen picked up a loose puck but as he circled around with it Judnick stole it and passed it out to Drobnick, who sailed by Duane and Fred like they were part of a shunning. He shot. He scored.

Norman's grin was wide as he congratulated his teammate. "Nice shot, Twicky!" he shouted through the cheers.

* * *

Jackie dashed down ice with the puck using every bit of energy his little body could muster. Norman came in, whacked it away from him, passed it agilely to Rossi who skated through Duane and Fred like they were paper bags, and rifled the puck into the net.

"Way to go, Rossi!" Jerry Norman yelled.

* * *

Chip passed the puck to Glen. Norman intercepted it handily, raced down ice and through Duane and Fred like they were invisible and scored in the peanut butter shelf. He flung his arms into the air, zooming around the net and into the waiting arms of his friends.

"Nice shot, Jer!" they praised. Corky Gunderson, the Eveleth goalie, yawned in his net.

* * *

Eveleth's Don Judnick shot from the corner. It zinged past Jackie's ear and over Duane, who tried to block it but fell. The puck hit the interior pipe, swung around inside the net and then rested in there, black and little. Cal, who had been an excellent puck stopper against every other team they had played, couldn't believe it.

The Eveleth team hugged.

When the trouncing was over the score was 9-1. Glen had managed the lone goal.

The sullen Thief River team, looking like cooked red lobsters, retreated to the dressing room and crashed on the benches. In the adjoining locker room, the Eveleth players could be heard celebrating their victory.

Beaten eyes greeted Coach Bedard as he entered the room. They weren't cocky anymore.

"Hey," Paul greeted them cheerfully, "keep your chins up, eh? It's only a game."

"When we get to high school we want to win the state championship..." a woeful Chip began to explain to Bedard. He couldn't go on.

Glen tried to pick up the thread, "...and if we can't beat Eveleth now..." his voice cracked and trailed off. Jackie picked it up. He was more mad than anything, "How can we beat them in high school?"

Duane, humiliated and red-eyed, sighed and turned over the stick he held on to, looking at Paul in pain and disgust. "They played like Fred and me wasn't even on the ice."

Paul sized up the situation and smiled warmly. "Listen guys," he sighed softly, "there's a lot to the game of hockey. They were good, damn good. The best I've ever seen at Pee Wee level. Between now and high school you guys will grow and you'll improve as players. How much is up to you and how hard you'll work. You've got to make your plow and pull it too."

He smiled sternly, but like a loving father warning his children, "You've got to pay the price if you want to be the best. Desire and hard work are *everything*. If you really want it and if you work as hard as you possibly can, I have every faith that you'll win that championship some day."

The atmosphere changed, hope transposed the pain. Bedard was not going to let the boys waste time on feeling sorry for themselves. "Now, let's go and get something to eat, eh?" he said in his Canadian accent.

10

making the plow

Glen, now fourteen, skated down ice with the puck the next winter after the Eveleth game. He was alone at the city park on an early winter morning. A thin gray mist hung about him.

He shot the puck, thumping the bottom board. Thud. The puck bounced off.

He hit it again. This time it hit the third board. Thud. "Darn," he exclaimed to himself.

He swirled back around the goal on the far end and slapped the puck toward the boards, hitting the bottom board again, cleanly. Thud.

When the puck bounced off he swooped in, picked up the puck with his stick, swirled long and low around the rink and came back hitting the boards again. This time he hit the second rung. Thud. He didn't smile, just looked grimly determined.

The puck rolled out to him from the boards and he slapshot it into the boards again, hitting the third board. This time he smiled.

Jim Hall and Fred walked up to the rink, hung over the boards and watched him as he smashed a wrist shot into the third board again. Thud. He frowned.

"Hey, Glen, whatcha doin'?" Jim called.

Glen took a break and looked solemnly at the inseparable duo, "Tryin' to hit each board all the way up and then all the way down."

Fred looked amazed. "I don't think anyone could ever do that."

Glen hit the puck, surely and accurately, into the bottom board again. "Someday I will," he answered.

* * *

When the boys were sophomores in high school a new boy moved to town. He had lived on a farm all his life, but his father died and his mother couldn't keep up the farm alone. His name was Rod Collins.

Rod had never played hockey but Rolle had lined the sophomore boys against the gym wall and hit pucks at them. Rod was the only boy who didn't flinch, so Rolle designated him back-up goalie for senior Jack Hoppe.

Glen and Chip, who were also sophomores that year, knew that

Rod needed more practice if he were to become a winning goalie, so with Rolle's help they devised a board with soap rubbed on it that they could shoot pucks off. Then they set Rod in front of a net in his driveway, put up their soap shooter and shot on him in the spring, summer and fall until the snow came.

Rod became the team goalie when he was a junior and Jack Hoppe had graduated. Rolle proudly told his friends that Rod had the fastest hands he'd ever seen in a goalie. That was the year of the eleven overtimes.

* * *

The determined boys played street hockey if the river or rinks were blocked with snow...

* * *

...and they scrimmaged on the river and on the town outdoor rink, practicing everything Paul Bedard had taught them.

11

back to good old 1955

The church clock gonged five times. Glen sat in the chair by the window in the room at the St. Paul Hotel. Jackie lay prone in the big bed. Both Jackie's and Glen's memories had time-traveled back and now the gongs jolted them forward to be encased in a present they didn't want.

Jackie gritted his teeth. A new sound and fresh determination reflected from his voice, a new strength of soul. "We'll come back next year and win, no matter what it takes."

Glen, gathering his own strength, looked out across the softly glittering predawn city and nodded.

12

new beginnings
November 1955

Rolle sat in the car for a minute before he joined the boys who waited for him by Long's Pond. The new hockey team was waiting for their first practice. The pond ice was sturdy enough to skate on for the few weeks before the arena ice was ready.

He involuntarily shuddered as he thought of his job for the year. There were just enough players for a shell of a team. They'd be lucky to win fifty percent of their games. It galled him to think that he had to take Jimmy and Cookie Reese onto the team. They hated him. They wouldn't mind him any more than rhinoceroses would. Jackie Poole could be a rabble-rouser, especially without Joey around to keep him in check, and Duane Glass could be a problem because he was so headstrong. Glen Carlson and Chip Strand were sterling.

Jackie, Glen and Chip would be the first line. It couldn't get much better than that.

Jim Hall, off Joey's line last year, would have to be coupled with the Reeses for the second line. He felt badly for Jim after having Joey and Sid as line mates.

Fred Dablow would have to play defense with Duane and they would be on the ice all the time. This was crazy. How could two boys hold up being on the ice all the time?

Rod would be the only goalie.

Art Cloutier, a new addition, would be the substitute. That was Rolle's complete team.

He thought back on last year and thought he would cry. Instead, he heaved a heavy sigh, climbed out of the car, got his sticks and skates out and ambled across the trampled-down frosted grass towards the boys. He was aware of his shoulders drooping and found himself looking at the sprinkling of recent snow that dusted the ground.

There was no place to sit so they stood for Rolle's first talk, given under the cool blue sky with ducks quacking in the background.

Rolle nodded at the boys and took a very deep breath. Then, assuming an all-business tone, he began, "We're under no illusions here. This year will be tough." He looked right at Jackie, who appeared to be very cocky and sure of himself. He was chewing gum loudly, smacking it and squinting through his glasses. Rod seemed to have mentally drifted off and Jimmy and Cookie looked insolent.

"We're a barebones team." He focused on Duane, "And I'm going to expect a lot out of you." Duane stood erect, looking formidable and very self-assured.

Covering his thoughts and fears with smooth professionalism, Rolle continued, "Everyone has to give one hundred percent."

Rolle fixed his gaze on giant Jimmy. His face was fierce, almost Neanderthal, and his nose looked like it had been broken. His clothes were too small for his newly huge frame, which must have grown four inches over the summer. Jimmy fidgeted with his stick. "Everyone has to keep the strict rules of no smoking..."

He was sure none of them smoked, but it was something he had to say.

Rolle looked over toward Glen, who listened attentively to his every word, "...and obeying the curfew. Ten o'clock weeknights, eleven weekends."

Rolle had never had a problem with curfew either. Thief River was a small town. Everyone in town knew about the curfew and someone was sure to report an errant athlete. Since it was an honor to be on the team, no one would take the chance.

He glanced at bright and sunny Chip, who stood like a racehorse at the gate, "Breaking those rules constitutes automatic suspension from the team." Rolle took a long breath and looked over the raggedy team and went on with his rules. His eyes moved to Fred next. Serious, respectful, quiet and ready Fred. He would have to work beyond his capabilities this year, Rolle thought, but he said, "No one can let up for a moment." He saw Jim, whose face was set with pure determination. It would be hard for Jim, Rolle reflected. He was so used to being with Joey and Sid. Rolle said, "You've got to do your job and help your teammate do his."

Then, flinching, Rolle looked over at Cookie and there was that shudder again. How would he ever keep this disrespectful and wild man-boy under control? Cookie responded by looking past him in a turned-off, disinterested, certainly disrespectful, manner. He had his, 'let's get this bullshit over with' look on his face. Oh, Lord, Rolle thought, the kid's not even going to try. Rolle's voice wavered a bit as he said, "We need to work very, very hard."

He met Art's eyes. If Cookie had Art's attitude they could go a long, long way together. Art was apprehensive. He wasn't the jock the rest were, but he was extremely bright, a quick learner, and would do what he was told. His eyes held to Rolle's, trying to gather strength from them. "It's up to you and your desire," Rolle continued.

He panned to Rod chewing his perpetual gum. Rod was serious, disciplined, ready. You could count on Rod. He was quick with his hands. Rod was also a daydreamer. He could drift from the net at the oddest times, out, out to the blue line, out to the red line. But Rod was a class act goalie when he put his mind to it, which he usually did.

"With hard work and a little luck we can win some games," Rolle intoned, feeling like a confused mallard with a nest of a duckling, a gosling, an egret...

They're not a team, he thought, looking at the group. They're so different. How can I ever form this funny mass into a team?

Rolle was a man with enormous pride. He certainly didn't want to face a year with a losing team. He was also a perfectionist who liked to win.

Rolle rubbed his hands together, like a genie rubbing a lamp, and said enthusiastically, "All right! Let's go!"

The boys jumped onto the ice and tore helter-skelter all over the pond. Cookie and Jimmy went booming off in one direction. Ducks scattered. Jackie, Glen and Chip hot-rodded it, blazing the puck between them. Duane took off in a different direction with his puck. Jim and Fred chased Duane. Rod just stood there.

Rolle blew his whistle and shouted as loudly as he could, "Over here. *Now!*" The boys looked disappointed but straggled in to shore. Cookie and Jimmy came slowest and last.

Rolle laced his voice with iron. "We are going to drill. No pucks. No sticks." The deflated boys tossed their sticks aside. Rolle boomed, "Start with the 'figure eight' drill."

The boys complied, but Cookie was grumpy.

"Dash drill," Rolle yelled, sergeant style.

Cookie glared at him.

The other boys looked confused by Rolle's treatment, but Glen, Duane, Jackie and Chip kept it going. Rolle had them do the 'circle' drill next and the boys were pooped.

"What's this bastard up to?" Cookie sputtered to Jimmy.

Rolle did not hear him.

"Alright now, 'burnout' drill," Rolle called almost cheerfully.

The unhappy, sweaty boys sullenly complied. No one talked. As they dragged off the ice after two hours of nonstop drills the sun dropped out of sight. Winded, and silently, they took off their skates and headed for their cars.

"Tomorrow, same time," Rolle called after them.

* * *

Rolle entered his modest home hangdog and droopy shouldered. He pulled off his rubber overshoes, hung his hat on a hook and peeled off his jacket.

"Anybody home?" he raised his voice a little but not too much as he walked dejectedly into the meticulous and cozy living room and plopped down onto the sofa.

"Be there in a minute, Dennis," a cheerful voice answered from somewhere in the house. Audry, Rolle's bubbly wife, came softly into the room followed by a two year old boy who crawled up onto Rolle's lap and threw his arms around his neck.

Audry kissed Rolle lightly and sat down beside him. "How was it?" she asked warily.

Rolle rolled his eyes up and sighed emphatically, "I don't think there's anything worse for a coach than facing a losing season after having such a powerhouse." The little boy eyed a stuffed animal on a chair and slid off Rolle's lap, wandering toward it. Audry looked at Rolle and questioned, "Did the Reese boys show up?"

Rolle rubbed his legs with fisted hands and whistled low, "Oooo yeah...and they don't have a clue about discipline or respect. It will just be a matter of time before a showdown with them." He closed his eyes and leaned his head back, frowning and pained, "I dread this season."

He rolled his head to face Audry and flatly continued, "How can I face the other coaches?"

"Can't someone else coach them, Dennis?"

"There's no one qualified and if there were, no one would do it."

The child came back with the stuffed animal in his possession. Rolle looked deep in concentration, "We just can't lose every game." He looked searchingly at Audry as he absently ruffled the boy's hair, still talking, "I'll have to pull out all the stops." He set his jaw and sat up firmly, talking in a low, smooth voice, "We'll have to drill and drill and drill...and those prima donnas won't like it."

13

pooles

A large platter of pork chops was passed around a utilitarian kitchen table squeezed and pressed to the gills with children and their father. A crowded configuration of crosses, madonnas, and other Catholic items adorned the walls. The petite, dark-haired mother dished up potatoes at the counter and then set the bowl on the table, along with a dish of peas and a leaning tower of Pisa stack of bread. Hands were everywhere, on everything. The dinner was clanky, noisy, filled with chatter and clatter.

Crashing though the back door, Jackie came grinning into the kitchen and then smiled specially at his mother, "Hi ma, I brought a few guys home for supper."

Jackie's dog bounced into the kitchen at the sound of his voice and jumped up on him. He hugged it while Mrs. Poole retrieved more plates from the cupboard.

Duane, Jim and Rod stomped loudly at the back entrance and piled into the kitchen. Mr. Poole looked up, "Good, good, just in time." The brood squeezed over to make room and the boys pulled up chairs and made themselves right at home, piling Matterhorns of mashed potatoes and loading thick pork chops onto their plates.

As Mrs. Poole sat down and picked up the bowl of peas, Mr. Poole asked, "So, how was practice boys?" The boys stopped eating and eyed each other.

Jackie cleared his throat and haltingly replied, "Um, fine."

Mrs. Poole reached for a pack of cigarettes and looked inside, "Elmer," she said to Mr. Poole, "have you been smoking my cigarettes?"

"No," Elmer swallowed, "why?" Mrs. Poole was staring inside her pack, "This was a new pack last night. I smoked one last night and thought I only smoked two today, and five are gone." She furrowed her brow and looked a little worried, "I must smoke unconsciously...I think I'm losing my mind..."

Jackie looked uncomfortable. Rod kicked him under the table. Jim tried to look as if he hadn't heard what she said.

Mr. Poole was about to answer her when the black phone on the wall rang startlingly loudly and the dog barked back at it. One of the smaller children reached for bread and knocked over his milk, letting out a wail. Mrs. Poole jumped up. The gravy boiled over on the stove. She ran to mop it up and the dog kept barking. The boys laughed.

"Get the milk for me, Liz," she asked, but Liz was already sopping it up.

Mr. Poole grabbed the phone, "Yes, operator..." he practically yelled over the outbreak of chaos, "...this is the Poole residence." He put his hand over the mouthpiece, "It's Joey!" he reported. He glowed, and then hurriedly began listening again, "Joey! Yes...yes...we'll be over to pick you up Wednesday night...how's school?" Mr. Poole listened and then said, "Good, good. How's hockey?" He listened again and beamed. "Fine, son. Fine! OK, good. See you Wednesday!" He hung up and said cheerfully, "It will be good for us to all be together for Thanksgiving." Then he added proudly, "Joey is doing very well at the University of North Dakota." Mrs. Poole smiled.

Jackie scowled. He thought when Joey went away that he, Jackie, would be in the limelight. But now it was Joey's college that lit up his parents' life.

14

point, break point

The morning after the first practice Glen and Chip wrestled themselves down the busy corridor to their lockers. As they hung up their hockey jackets and got their books, Rod walked up and said quietly, "How are you guys anyway?"

Glen and Chip grimaced. Chip whispered, "Stiff."

Jimmy and Cookie swaggered by but they weren't in any pain. "See you guys later," Jimmy said without smiling.

The three huddled and Glen talked low, "Rolle never did anything like this last year. What's gotten into him anyway?"

* * *

It was after school of the second day of practice. The boys dragged themselves to the shore of Long's Pond. When they got there Rolle was skating on the smooth, clear ice. Rolle rarely skated so it was novel for the boys to watch him. He was a fine skater and they thought this was a good sign.

The boys hustled into their gear on the shore. "I guess Rolle was just crabby yesterday," Glen observed.

"Yeah," Chip shot back. "He looks good today." He ran his fingers over his rockered skates. "He probably feels terrible about how he treated us yesterday."

"I guess we'll be scrimmaging," Jackie offered.

With renewed vigor they grabbed their sticks and hit the ice jovially, throwing pucks down and starting around the ice stick handling.

Rolle blew his whistle in an insistent manner. The cheerful boys gathered around him quickly, except for Cookie who skated up casually in his 'I'll do as I please when I please' attitude. Rolle chose to ignore this. He didn't smile when he looked at the boys. He didn't even look pleasant.

Jackie felt uneasy.

"You won't need your sticks," he instructed sternly.

The boys looked wary as they tossed their sticks onto the bank.

"We'll start with 'dump and chase'," he continued with a voice of unmistaken reign. "Then we'll do the 'figure eight', then the 'circle', and then the 'burnout'." He positioned himself a little away from the group and put his whistle between his teeth.

Cookie skated lazily off for the drills with Jackie, "This guy's an ass."

Jackie nodded.

The boys worked to exhaustion as the sun sank. When it settled itself away Rolle finally called them in. They came, fully spent and gasping for breath.

On the dark shore of the pond he directed, "We have less than four weeks until our season opener...and a lot of work to be done. We've got to improve and work a little harder every day. We have a long way to go to become mediocre so we can at least win half our games."

It was dark now so no one could see anyone else's expression.

* * *

Cookie, Jackie, Art, Chip and Glen sat doggedly in Miss Skomedahl's English class, grouped together in the rear of the classroom working on an assignment. They had been through Rolle's boot camp for two weeks now and were about fed up.

Gray haired Miss Skomedahl sat behind her desk in front, busy with something. Miss Skomedahl was always busy and believed everyone else should be too. She wore a prim gray dress with a lace collar and a warm black sweater around her shoulders.

Miss Skomedahl's students loved her for challenging them, for bringing a new dimension to their lives, and for really believing that they could learn the difficult material she covered, which was more college-level English material than high school. She brought the English language and classical literature to life.

On the bulletin board behind her a large poster read, "Turnabout Dance, Friday, Dec. 22."

The hockey players' thoughts were not on their assignment and she was aware of that. She would give them a minute to get it out of their systems before she clamped down.

Chip leaned forward in his desk, "Think he'll let us use pucks and sticks today?"

Glen answered dryly, "Don't get your hopes up."

Jackie's face twisted, "Two weeks of drills! Christ! We need scrimmages. He's treating us like babies."

Chip's eyes widened in terror like a child watching a horror movie, "We can't let the championship slip between our fingers like this.

We're wastin' time. Eveleth's not wastin' time."

The boys looked seasick.

Duane peered over his book and snapped, "We're winnin' with or without Rolle. Don't anyone forget it."

Miss Skomedahl looked up and smiled wryly, "Is Mr. Poole done with his work?"

Jackie's paper was totally blank and everyone knew it. "Not quite," he answered.

The class broke out in laughter and the boys knew this was their cue to get busy.

* * *

During lunch break on the same day, cute, demure Angie and her full-figured friend strolled down the hall, holding their school books at chest level. Suddenly Angie's friend nudged her in the side urgently, "There he is."

Glen and Chip, still aching from practice, walked stiffly as they came toward the girls in the people-current they were in, but being jostled by the students going the other direction. They didn't notice these girls or anything around them as they talked to each other.

"I've heard of male menopause," Chip ventured. "Do you think that's what's wrong with Rolle?"

Angie, unaware of Glen and Chip's conversation but realizing Glen didn't notice her, squeezed her books, "I don't think I can do it."

Her girlfriend insisted, "Come on. He'll go. I know he will."

Angie protested, "What if he says 'No'?"

Glen and Chip started to pass them as Glen was answering Chip, "It's a possibility he could be, I guess..." but was interrupted because Angie mustered up her courage and stepped in front of them.

"Glen?"

Glen looked over at Chip and hesitated, awkwardly.

Angie, temporarily mute, was stabbed with a pencil by her plump friend. She looked at the floor and said very fast, "Will you go to the dance with me?"

Glen was completely taken aback. He felt like he didn't have any air inside of him. Angie's friend puckered her lips and smiled behind a pair of ersatz diamond glasses. Chip looked over at her, amused, and nudged Glen back to his senses. Glen, in front of a roving mass of students and teachers, in essence for a teenager, his world, blushed.

Angie looked up at him and Glen found himself captivated with the deep blue eyes and beauty of this girl. He realized quickly that he would be a fool to miss this chance.

"Uh," he articulated artlessly to Angie, "Sure."

* * *

Rolle's practices remained monotonously the same. Drills. For the first time, practice had moved inside to the old arena where the Thieves played when the boys were kids. The arena had not changed. The tin seemed to hold the cold in, it was still small and people still had to stand to watch the games.

The boys had given up trying to outguess Rolle.

Coach Rolle held his team meeting on the ice. He spoke to a despondent, edgy, itchy, unhappy bunch. "We have one week until our opening game."

Jackie remarked under his breath to Cookie, "Then why the hell aren't we scrimmaging?"

Rolle didn't hear Jackie and slapped his hands together zestily, feigning enthusiasm, "All right, let's go!"

The boys broke halfheartedly and skated out to warm up.

As Glen circled the rink Duane skated up to him and snarled, "What's wrong with you, Carlson?"

"What?" Glen looked startled.

Duane glared him fully in the eye, a disgusted sort of look, like looking at pus in a wound. "Taking up with a dame when we have serious work to do. You tryin' to blow our chances?"

His skates scraped angrily off before Glen could answer.

The practice consisted of a series of Rolle blowing his whistle, 'one on one' drills, Rolle flagging the boys back, 'knee drops' for Rod, skating hard and passing drills. Cookie lazily overpassed to Jim. Rolle blew his whistle.

"Try harder, Cookie!" Rolle's voice was edged in acid. "I don't want any laziness out here. Do it again." Cookie scowled.

The rest of that practice went pretty much the same way.

* * *

After practice the disgruntled boys headed for the Rexall drug store. There really wasn't anywhere else to go and Mr. Ekren, the owner-pharmacist, was always friendly to them. They ordered sodas and made themselves at home in the huge back booth. A Prowler schedule was tacked up on the wall.

Jackie sat hunched and glowering behind the table, "What's

wrong with Rolle? Three weeks of drills..."

Cookie sneered and stretched his lumberjack neck, "Rolle doesn't know hockey. We need a good coach."

Jackie stared down his lime freeze like it was solely responsible.

Two town businessmen sauntered up to the counter. One called over jokingly, "Well! If it isn't the hockey players! Sorry you missed on State last year when you had your chance. It will be a pretty grim year without Joey."

Being the darlings of the town last year, this was pretty hard for the boys to take. No one had chided them, ever.

The other businessman chuckled and ran his thick tongue across his lip, adding, "Just keep your heads up! We can't always be winners all the time."

Jackie gaped blackly into his freeze. He felt cool hatred for the men. The other boys wriggled uncomfortably. Cookie dared them with his stare but the men didn't actually look their way.

Jackie whispered to Cookie, "Let's get outta here. I want a smoke." Jackie and Cookie slipped out, leaving their staring comrades behind.

"I thought Jackie wasn't smoking anymore." Glen sounded concerned.

"If he gets caught it's curtains for us," Rod responded gloomily.

* * *

Elmer Poole closed his business, the Viking Bar, for the evening. He put the sign in the window and locked the door. Jackie sat sullenly on a barstool in the clean, quiet bar that was ready to open the next day.

Elmer, turning out the lights, said, "OK, Jackie, we can go home now." He began to walk by, then hesitated, looking at his glum child. "What's wrong, son?"

Jackie's eyes misted as he struggled to form the words, then he blurted clumsily, "Will I ever be as good as Joey?" His father reached out to him and put a well-worked hand on his shoulder. He spoke gruffly, tender eyes betraying a deep love for this son that was so different from Joey. "You already are, Jackie."

Jackie pulled away and put his head in his hands, "Joey got All State last year. I can't get it if we don't get to State and all Rolle does is drill us all the time." He looked into his father's eyes; the usual fidgetiness had fled. "Dad, we can't win if we don't scrimmage," his chest hurt from holding back the tears. "It's not fair."

Elmer hugged him, "You've got to get along with your coach, son."

Jackie let himself be hugged. He wanted to become part of his father's peace, his strength, but he answered belligerently, "He doesn't know hockey as well as I do, Dad."

* * *

The team dressed in the freshly painted Thief River Falls locker room.

"Shit," Jackie muttered under his breath as he banged things around while he got ready. He was the team captain and felt personally responsible for the fate of his team. It only added to the anxious mood that had accumulated from the first day at Long's Pond.

Everyone else was quiet until Rod, feebly breaking the heavy silence with a false note of cheerfulness, offered, "Well, shall we go up?"

Chip answered hastily, "We'd better! Rolle's waitin'!"

The boys tramped heavily up the sterile stairwell and then skated out onto the ice where Rolle, the coach enemy, was waiting. They began to skate around the rink.

The shrill whistle called, and the boys automatically stopped skating to await instructions. Rolle called out, "OK, let's get started with the 'figure eight' drill."

The boys fell into the drill.

Rolle waited a few minutes, then blew his whistle again and yelled lustily, "Wind sprints!"

The boys lined up on the blue line. Jackie's jaw was tight, his breath uneven. He looked mad.

Rolle waited until they finished the wind sprints and then sounded his whistle again, "Starts and stops!"

Jackie had had it. In a red flash of unchecked anger, he flung his hockey stick against the wall. It smashed into the clock, shattering the glass, and sent it smashing against the concrete floor. "I'm sick of this bullshit!" he screamed explosively at the top of his lungs, looking straight at a shocked Rolle. The other players looked on, pale as pole cats as Jackie shook with rage.

Rolle's face turned the color of mashed strawberries as he skated over to Jackie, screaming, "What the hell are you doing?"

Jackie stood his ground, screaming back, completely out of control, "It's our life! Our whole damn life!" Tears streamed down his panicked face, "You don't give a shit whether we win or lose!"

Rolle was shaking and talking without moving his lips, in an unsuccessful attempt to cover a surge of wrath, "We've got to drill..."

Jackie screamed so loud his voice trailed up an octave echoing around the arena, "To hell with drills!" Jackie stood on the barren ice, completely over the edge, "We play games, not drills!"

Rolle looked at him coldly, "Another outburst like that and you can turn in your equipment." Rolle struggled for composure as he skated up close to Jackie. He put a shaky hand on his star center's shoulder and looked at him squarely. Rolle talked quietly, finding an inner strength he didn't know he had. "I know it's hard for you, Jackie. It's hard for me, too. My ass is on the line here."

Jackie's cheeks streamed with tears; he looked vulnerable and afraid. Rolle continued, eyes still on Jackie's, "I know we need a miracle here but it needs to be backed up by all the hard work we can muster and I know you're not afraid of that."

Rolle abruptly turned and skated away blowing the whistle again, addressing all the boys in a louder than usual tone, "All right boys, ten laps around and then 'starts and stops'."

Jackie turned on his skates, taking off furiously around the ice. The others followed.

15

decision

The mellow golden lights that hung over the street punctuated the pitch black sky as the flattened little Prowler team, hauling its gear, exited the ice arena. Stealthily and quietly as huge gray wolves they slid around the edge of the arena to the backside. Deserted buildings backed up to the arena so it was dark and quiet and safe.

The pack formed a silent ring around Jackie, who shakily lit up a cigarette.

Rod began in a soothing voice, "You OK, Jackie?"

Jackie sucked in a drag and answered in a voice not much more than a whisper, "Yeah."

He could sense the deep concern of his ice buddies. Odd, he didn't even hang out with these guys. In fact, he had only one friend at school, Ross Sloane. Ross didn't play hockey.

Jackie's life was a mess and he knew it. He was wild, a braggart at school, a showoff who was barely passing his classes, brash to his peers, and most of the teachers didn't understand this bright but odd, self-destructing renegade.

Worse, he had a crush on pretty, sweet Laurie and didn't even have the courage to ask her out.

But on his team he was the undisputed leader.

The kids at school liked him, but he was on the outside because he was so wild. He could step in the ring but he didn't. All it would have taken was for him to stop smoking and clean up his act. The ring had a space for him, the ring wanted him, but he elected to prowl the outside not a lone wolf, but more an injured one.

Duane was a lone wolf and a survivor at school. Duane didn't smoke. Duane was tough as hell, but a law unto himself. He knew himself. He did the good grades thing and got along without compromising himself.

"Yeah," he said again. "I'm OK." Jackie dragged long, held a few seconds, then blew it out.

The boys gave him time.

Then he spoke, low and controlled, "Rolle's talkin' about winnin' some games so we don't lose face...so we can be mediocre. He just doesn't understand that we've got to be a winning team...all the way."

He looked at Glen and Chip, "He scrimmaged us all the time last year.

That's all we did, scrimmage, scrimmage, scrimmage! Now we're a week to our first game and we haven't had one scrimmage."

The group stood quiet.

Duane broke the silence. His voice was determined and confident and calm, "We'll scrimmage on our own, then. Before school, and on weekends on the river and the town rink."

The grave boys looked at Duane and then nodded in agreement,

Jackie squashed his cigarette butt.

Jimmy, the craggy no-nonsense rock who rarely spoke, answered, "Ain't nothin' more important than winnin' State."

And so it happened there, behind an old arena, in an inauspicious alley next to the garbage cans, that each boy felt a curious resoluteness, a gluing at-one-ness with each other and a choking sense of warmness that they were never able to talk about together.

They didn't know it but they had just laid the first block of the camaraderie of the 1956 Prowler team firmly in place.

16

all work and no play

It was early December, the day after the decision. The river was frozen solidly and the cold spilled out of Canada into the town. The sun peeked over the flat rim of the city, bringing the frosty dawn. There was no snow yet.

School books and boots lined the brown shores of the river. The scant Prowler team practiced.

Cookie passed the puck to his brother, who shot long and hard on Rod. The puck cruised past Rod into the sticks. Glen and Chip raced in and talked to Rod, who nodded. Jimmy shot again, his powerful arms sending the puck toward Rod. Rod yelled back in earnest anger, "What're you trying to do, kill me?"

The boys practiced until the last minute they dared, then ran for their cars and piled into them, roared off to school, crammed their skates, jackets and sticks in their lockers and sped for their classes as the bell rang. No one knew what they were up to or what their dream was. A veil had gone up around the boys.

After school was practice with Rolle and his drills. With the new self-imposed direction they settled in and made use of every drill, every minute on the ice. Endurance, strength, skill. They must have those to win, too.

One day during a '60 second' drill, Cookie skated up to Jackie and leaned over to him to say something. Rolle blew his whistle long and shrill. "You're not hustling!" he yelled. "Get off the ice until you mean business." The boys piled onto benches and sat silently seething until Rolle let them on again.

Another time Art was practicing defense with Fred, skating backwards and trying to stop Chip from getting through them. Art drifted out. The annoying whistle sounded. "Stay with it, Art!" Rolle boomed. "Do it again."

Always the whistle, always the drills. Always the repeats. Rolle was on them, never letting up. Practice was the hated time of the day but it was endurable because afterwards they would scrimmage.

Then home for supper and, as soon as their mothers were satisfied they had eaten enough, it was off to the lighted city rink to practice. Thieves players joined the boys, pushing them past their limits.

One night Chip, Jackie and Glen skated down ice. It was crisp out, the kind of cold that made them feel refreshed and raring to go. The Thieves' defensemen came in to thwart them.

Jackie had the puck and passed it to Chip without looking. He knew in his bones exactly where Chip was. Chip flicked the puck past Rod's glove. Chip grinned, Jackie nodded back exhilarated.

Suddenly Jackie threw his stick over the boards yelling, "Pum pum pullaway!" as he dashed for center ice. All the skaters forgot what they were doing. Sticks flew over the boards like matches in an explosion as a line formed quickly on the side of the ice.

Jackie yelled, "Pum pum pullaway!" again and like chargers in an old battle the boys tried to get past Jackie. He flew after Fred, nailed him and quickly tagged Art.

Then, back to center ice accompanied by Fred and Art, he yelled again, "Pum pum pullaway!" and the charge was on again with Fred and Art added as the pesky taggers. Jackie loved being on the ice. It was the only time he seemed not to be in trouble. His mind was clear there. He was in his element, on his turf, in his heaven. He didn't make mistakes on the ice. His mind was at rest. He was safe there.

Some Saturday mornings found the boys in the road in front of Duane's house playing hockey on the ice-paved street using an ice chunk for a puck. When a car drove by sliding into the ruts, the boys patiently moved out of the way.

Every morning, every day after school, every evening after supper, every weekend for hours on end they practiced, practiced, practiced.

* * *

At dinner one night, Rolle's wife Audry asked him how the team was going. He had seemed happier and she felt it was a safe subject to broach. His fork, spun full with spaghetti, stopped midway from plate to mouth and he actually smiled as he looked at it and then her.

"They've really been working hard and their attitude is all work," he mused. Rolle was unaware of the boy's plan to win State and unaware of their self-imposed working scrimmages.

"I think they can make mediocre." He shoved the noodles in his mouth, looking satisfied. "With how few of them there are, I can live with that," he added.

17

school days

Rod, Glen, Chip, Fred and Jim, wearing their hockey jackets, rushed up the wide stairs toward the big rear doors of Lincoln High carrying books and skates. They had just passed Duane and Gordon Bredeson, a friend of Duane's, wading through deep snow on the football field, toting a door. Jim was still looking in their direction, mumbling, "What're they doing?" as Fred pulled him inside by the sleeve of his jacket and emphatically remarked, "We probably don't want to know!" The boys chuckled as they entered the school.

As they shoved their jackets and skates into lockers, Jackie ran screeching down the hall, "Someone bring the history assignment!"

Art, Glen, Jackie, Chip, and Rod entered study hall together and proceeded to the back of the room. Duane rushed in at the last minute looking very pleased with himself. Cookie was already there.

Rod leaned over to Duane and whispered, "Where have you been?"

Duane gloated, "Gordy and I stole the library door. They won't find it until spring."

Duane leaned over to a moon-faced girl blowing her nose, sitting kitty corner from him. He flashed his winning smile, "Hey, is my homework done?"

She quickly removed her hanky from sight, fluffed up her pincurled hair and smiled back at him coyly, "Almost."

Duane looked away from her as he distractedly answered, "Good."

Jackie desperately moaned, "Who's got the history assignment?"

Cookie looked up at him, bored. "Who cares about a history assignment? We've got a game tonight."

Glen whispered to Rod, "You ready for tonight?"

Rod sat up straight and twisted back to look at Glen. "You'd better believe it!"

The loudspeaker at the front of the classroom crackled. The moon faced girl handed Duane his assignment, but before he reached for it, Jackie intercepted in mid-transit. Duane let it go and sarcastically whined, "You really should get your homework done on time, Jackie," but Jackie was already copying the assignment.

The loudspeaker crackled again and then Mr. Ostby's voice came on. "Your attention for the announcements, please. The Prowlers play the Grand Forks Indians at the arena tonight. Good luck in your season opener, boys." He paused, then continued, "Girls...get your tickets for the turnabout dance before noon."

Jackie fluttered his eyes and begged Glen in a high, sing-song Scarlett O'Hara voice, "Oh, Glen, will you take me to the dance?" He ducked when Glen raised a pencil to clobber him, but Glen nailed him anyway.

The loudspeaker sounded muffled, like someone had their hand over it, then Mr. Ostby's voice returned, this time terse and loud. "Duane Glass and Gordy Bredeson return the library door immediately!"

Duane's swallowed-a-cat look changed to dumbfounded. The whole class laughed the happy gut-splitting laughter of kids who liked each other.

18

trouble

Inside the Lincoln High basketball locker room, Mr. Boynton, the burly basketball coach, twirled a basketball on his finger while he listened to the announcements. He snarled as he looked up at Mr. Addison, his scruffy blonde assistant, "They'll get tromped this year." He smiled an introverted, satisfied smile. "There's only ten of 'em. One's nothin' better than a bench warmer and those two new brutes will give Rolle too much trouble to be of much use." He narrowed his eyes darkly, "It's time for those sassy brat hockey players to eat crow!" He slapped his tall lanky assistant across the back. The assistant parroted his mean grin.

19

out the starting gate

The meager Prowler team gathered in the old arena locker room gearing up for the Grand Forks game. The team was so sparse that they spaced themselves like first class airline passengers, spreading their equipment around them like spoiled children. The school board had unexpectedly voted funds for a new set of white jerseys. They were white with bold black letters cascading down the front diagonally that read, "PROWLERS".

As Rod pulled on his new jersey, he noticed Chip having a tough time getting his very rockered skates on. "What's wrong with your skates, Chipper?"

Chip tried to act nonchalant as he barely squished his foot in, but his eyes reflected pain. "Nothin'. Just getting a little tight I guess."

Rod looked at the small skate and the bigger-than-the-skate foot. "You've got to get bigger skates, Chip. Those are at least two sizes too small."

Chip's eyes locked Rod's and there was sadness but he was also resigned, "There's nothin' I can do about it, Rod. There's no time to work, you know that."

Rolle, wearing a snappy bow tie, entered the locker room unceremoniously. He had to give a good pep talk, Lord knew they needed it. Grand Forks had a strong, tough team.

Art fidgeted with his hockey stick, twirling it on end. Chip thumped his pained feet absently. Jimmy sat with his back against the cement brick wall with a dreamy, faraway look in his eyes. Cookie assumed his 'this-is-not-important' look of disdain and disinterest for Rolle's benefit. He flashed Rolle an insolent stare that Rolle was becoming masterful at ignoring. Duane was poker faced, Glen intent, Fred and Jim resolute.

Rolle put a foot up on one of the benches and began, "We find out tonight what we can do. It's important to win our first game. You are skating for the state of Minnesota and they are skating for North Dakota. Remember your pride in skating for your state. Grand Forks Central has talent and strength. So do we. If you play it smart you can take these guys. Don't take any stupid penalties." He looked slightly apprehensive. "Let's get out there and skate our tails off!"

Inside the arena, students hung over the boards pounding and cheering as the teams warmed up. The spectators in the first row had arrived two hours early for their good places. Since there was no plexiglass, the die-hard first rowers ducked sticks and dodged pucks.

Jimmy and Cookie's large family, the Reeses, stood in the crowd. The parents were tall and dressed in rough, clean clothes. The clan was attentive and quiet. Next to them stood the Poole flock, all bundled up from head to toe. Father Noah, dressed in his robes and a heavy black coat, hovered nearby. Chip's and Rod's mothers came together and were both nervous. Both women had it very hard financially; Rod's mother was a fairly recent widow and Chip's father had died of cancer when Chipper was eighteen months old.

The Halls, the Dablows, the Glasses and the Carlsons stood by the other families. They were pillars-of-the-town type households with comfortable homes and good incomes.

No one knew what to expect with this first game.

Elmer Poole leaned over to Mr. Reese, "Your boys look awfully good out there, Reese."

Mr. Reese nodded and added roughly, "It was damn tough for 'em not being on the team last year."

Elmer sympathetically answered, "I know it was."

The team was in the box and the old jitters were back.

"Remember, Fred, don't let them split us," Duane reminded him as they skated to their positions. "If they can't get through us, they can't score." Fred nodded.

The game was on. Jackie won the face off. The crowd cheered. Jackie skated down ice and passed the puck to Glen who slid it over to Chip, who shot. The goalie made the save. The action was not thrilling at first, but it was picking up momentum.

A Grand Forks player had the puck and was skating for all he was worth along the boards with his head down. Chip hesitated slightly, then smashed the player into the boards. The crowd roared in approval.

Mrs. Strand looked on in amazed disgrace. "For shame, Chipper," her little shrill voice yelled above the crowd.

"He's supposed to do that," Mr. Glass told her, "It's part of the game, Palma. Remember I told you that last year?" The players and fans on both teams chuckled. This dialogue went on every year.

Later, Jimmy lost the face off to the Grand Forks Indians. As the opponent passed the puck, Jimmy's stick zapped out and intercepted it. Rolle noticed the intense concentration as Jimmy lumbered toward the net. His huge frame, not just his arms, shot with all its strength. The puck forced its way past the goalie and into the net.

Father Noah yelled and jumped around, his long robes dancing. J.C., back as Rolle's volunteer assistant again this year, was ecstatic. Cookie, Jimmy and Jim hugged on the ice. The Reese family exploded into a happy melee while the Poole family leaned over the boards, pounding.

Later in the game, feisty Jim Hall sat in the penalty box watching Chip skate backwards. A Grand Forks player was going to pass. Chip sensed this intuitively, stopped, reversed direction, intercepted the pass, and kept going with it. He turned on his afterburners, skirted the defense, faked out the goalie, flipped the disc into the net, then flew out of control and crashed into the boards behind the net. The crowd roared.

Chip's mother, a little bit of a thing, cheered a little chirp.

The game wound on. With one minute left in the game the score was 3-2. Jackie had scored for the Prowlers.

Rolle talked to his team very excitedly, "We've got to hold them. Duane and Fred, stay in your positions. Don't go chasing around." He looked to Chip, "Stay in control. You're going to get hurt smashing against the boards like that."

The Grand Forks coach motioned the goalie off. Another player skated on and took his place. Six against five, but it left no goalie to protect the Grand Forks net.

The last minute was played tough and gritty by both teams. Neither team scored. The game ended 3-2, Thief River Falls.

Inside the locker room the Prowlers got out of their sweaty gear. Jackie slammed his helmet down angrily, "We played like shit. It's a miracle we won."

Duane, dead serious and commanding, growled, "Looks like we'll be doing some serious practicin' over Christmas vacation."

* * *

The basketball coach and his assistant pulled out of the parking lot after the game. Folks were walking by going to their cars. "They barely got by this team. The others'll clean 'em and fry 'em," he gloated.

20

dances, girls, skates

Miss Skomedahl stood authoritatively behind her desk at the front of the room. The same poster about the dance was still behind her on the bulletin board, and written on the chalkboard behind her was FRIDAY, DECEMBER 22. A decorated Christmas tree graced the corner. An upbeat, warm and satisfied mood permeated the class.

"Pass your Beowulf test forward now please, class," she requested. Jackie groaned. His classmates snickered. As the English students passed their papers in she added, "After Christmas we'll be memorizing three hundred lines of Shakespeare. Anyone who wants a head start can be working on them over Christmas vacation." She smiled warmly at the class who respected her so much, "We've accomplished a great deal this semester. Have a happy holiday."

The stunned hockey players looked at each other in shock.

"Did she say three hundred lines?" Rod paled.

"Of *Shakespeare*?" Chip piped in.

Jackie's eyes twinkled as he feigned seriousness. "Well, guys, Glen can't go to the dance tonight. He'll have to stay home and memorize Shakespeare."

"Whose gonna teach you how to dance, Carlson?" Duane goaded.

Jackie leaned forward in his desk, "Let a girl talk you into this and, wham, they've got you around their little finger..." The bell rang to signal the end of class.

Glen smiled, "You guys are just jealous."

"There is no way I can learn three hundred lines," Rod muttered miserably to himself as they milled out of class.

Duane turned to Cookie, "You guys goin' tonight, Cook?"

"Nah," Cookie answered. "Jimmy and me don't have time for girls. We're building our stock car for next summer."

* * *

A golden Christmas tree ornament hung on a green tree branch. Reflections of dancers could be seen on it. Next to the tree, the kids browsed through a stack of records by a phonograph. Elvis' "Blue Suede Shoes" rocked in the background. The auditorium was crammed full of energetic dancers. A row of chairs lined the perimeter with coats thrown over the backs. This casual dance was charged with a good time atmosphere. The boys wore "good" jeans and the girls, full skirts that swirled to their waists when they twirled, revealing stacks of full slips.

The hockey players, sans Glen, Cookie and Jimmy, formed a knot at the door. Glen and Angie entered. Jackie, in his girl voice, sang out intimidatingly, "Oh look everyone! It's Glen and..." he paused, then with great emphasis, "*Angie*." The boys glared at them.

Glen awkwardly guided Angie past the guys, flipping Jackie off behind his back.

Angie, not expecting this and embarrassed almost to tears, looked the other way. They wove their way in and threw their coats over the backs of a chair and stood uncomfortably watching the other dancers.

The song ended and strains of "My Prayer" filled the auditorium. "You wanna dance?" Glen queried bumblingly. Angie nodded.

Was this a terrible mistake? Glen wondered. Was this girl wishing she had asked someone else? Glen pulled Angie close and they started dancing to the crooning of The Platters and Angie was definitely glad she had come with Glen.

The boys at the door watched sourly.

* * *

Christmas vacation. The boys were taking full advantage of the time, and the weather, to practice.

Angie and her friends, out skating, glided down the river hopping over the cracks and avoiding the little patches of hard snow that packed together. Angie, dressed in a scarlet coat, leaned on a friend for support over a choppy patch. She looked up and spotted Glen playing hockey in the distance. Haltingly, she pleaded to her companions, "Let's go the other direction."

The girl she held on to replied, "They see us. It will look funny if we don't go on now."

Chip was in the process of merrily passing the puck to Glen when the girls came upon them. Glen, mouth half open in the presence of Angie, stared at her as she and her friends skated past. Distracted, he let out a surprised "ooph" as the puck socked him in the stomach. The other boys looked over at him, disgusted. Duane stiffened and turned his back, as if he were performing a formal ostracism.

Glen scrambled for the puck too late. Jimmy picked it up and skated down ice, passing to Cookie who bulldozed by Art and fired on

Rod, but missed the net altogether. The puck slid on out of sight down the river. They all watched, laughing.

Chip skated to the side of the river, sat down and pulled his skates off. He looked at his feet sadly and started rubbing them; they were dead white from the too-small skates. Rod, who had followed Chip to the river's edge, watched him massage them.

"Jesus, Chipper. Is there some way to get new skates?"

Chip continued rubbing his cramped toes, "I'm savin' up but with us practicin' all the time I have so little time to work at the grocery store. As it is, I already have to give my mom whatever I make to pay bills."

Rod sat down beside Chip on the long dead grass. "Your ma can't afford to help, can she?"

Chip stopped rubbing for a moment and looked back at Rod, "We barely have food on the table."

* * *

Vast expanses of frozen prairie stretched endlessly in all directions. It was desolate, quiet and strangely separate from the rest of the world. The sun was setting on the bare ground that should have been covered with snow. It was two nights before Christmas and the night after the dance.

Inside Chip's beat-up old Chevy, Chip, Jackie, Rod and Duane drove down a deserted dirt road. Glen had taken Angie to a movie.

Jackie was smoking in pure peace.

Chip rolled down the window and yelled, "Hey world, move over! Here come the champions!"

* * *

A Christmas tree sat on a table in the corner of the drab living room of the house Chip's mother rented. A smattering of wrapped packages sat under it. The furniture was brown, the worn carpet tan with the walls a soft beige. The highlight of the room was a set of handsome high school graduation pictures of Chip's six older sisters and one older brother that proudly adorned the wall.

Rod and Chip sat in the adjoining kitchen at the large round oak table with a half a plate of delicious Swedish cookies on it. Their Shakespeare books were opened as they munched the Christmas goodies. Chip's hockey gear aired out in one corner, but his too-small skates and stick were near the door. "Deck the Halls" was just finishing up on KTRF. The announcer's voice came over the waves wishing everyone a happy day before Christmas, then Elvis sang a Christmas song.

"Try it again, Rod, I know you can get it," Chip said patiently as he leaned over the table and plopped another cookie in his mouth. "We can't win without us on the team and we can't play if we don't pass English." He looked back at the book, "Fair..."

Rod sighed, "Fair is foul, and foul is fair. Hover through the, the...fog and...fog and..." He looked desperate, "I can't do this."

"We all can and we will," Chip clipped plaintively. "We have two and a half months to learn the lines. Every day we have to learn four lines. If we do it together it won't be so hard. Now let's..."

The phone rang, filling the tiny house with its importance. Chip answered cheerfully, "Strands."

He listened. "Yeah, this is Chipper Strand," he answered to the silence.

"What?" His voice got louder, "*What?* You're kidding!" He listened again. "You bet I'll be right there!"

He hung up the phone, jumped into the air and let out a war whoop as he grinned ear to ear.

"Who was that?" an astonished Rod asked.

"Oh, Rod! You'll never believe this!" He looked at his friend like he was going to burst into zillions of pieces. "Someone from town bought me a pair of new skates. I'm supposed to go to the sport shop and get fitted!" Tears of joy rolled down his face.

"What are we waiting for?" Rod hollered jumping up and grabbing his jacket, "Let's go!"

* * *

Christmas Day found the boys on the river. The sun sparkled and so did they. The thing to do was try out new skates, so "everyone" was on the river. Fathers took their youngsters and an old kitchen chair and headed for the ice. Groups of teenagers went together. Young married people skated up the river. The old push sleds with runners were revived with the newest babies in them. There was minimal snow so they could skate as far as they dared. Bonfires lined the shore for skaters to stop and warm up.

The hockey team had marked off its territory on the smoothest section of the river. Everyone stayed clear.

All the former hockey players home for the holidays came to skate with the boys, including those who currently played hockey at college:

Joey, Darrell Durgin and Bobby Helgeland were home from the University of North Dakota, Lyle Guttu from Harvard, Marv Jorde and Mike McMahon from the University of Minnesota, and Jack Hoppe, home from the service. Local Thieves players, including Bedard, Dorn, and Swede Lund joined in the fun and that river never saw a better hockey day. Chip played without pain, tearing up the hard, cold ice. He felt bold and free. His smile warmed them up better than any bonfire.

Bill Froiland, the kind man from Chip's Lutheran Church who had anonymously given Chip his skates, watched from the bridge and understood the true joy of giving.

hallock

The snow came and didn't stop. The town was buried deep in it. Surrounded by high drifts of crystal snow, a large two-story house had been dug out of its foundation. Three long steel beams were in place under the house. Cookie, Jimmy and Mr. Reese, working in t-shirts and jeans, muscles bulging from beneath, shoved huge timbers crosswise under the steel beams, an effort that required tremendous brute strength.

A truck was parked in front of the house, with an A-frame winch in front of it. Enormous house jacks were placed on the side. It was a nasty, wind-whipped day.

Mr. Reese grunted under the strain, "Looks like we've about got it, boys."

Cookie strained his muscles to the popping point to get the timber under the house, "Good. We've got 'bout half an hour to catch that bus to Hallock."

* * *

The drafty Lincoln High bus carried the Prowlers down a dark, drifting road. It propelled them into country so howling lonesome and black it seemed midnight. But in January in the upper reaches of Minnesota, it was only five o'clock in the afternoon.

Inside the bus "Rock Around the Clock" sporadically spurted on and off through Fred's transistor radio, which he held to the iced window for better reception. Most everyone else clowned around. Occasionally a wadded-up piece of paper shot out in the dark, hitting the bus ceiling, the back of a seat or someone's head. Jimmy and Cookie sat distinguished unto themselves, within themselves, slouched down, arms crossed. They weren't jokesters and they certainly didn't hurl bits of paper around dark buses.

Glen made funny faces and yelled up to the bus driver, "You'll probably get lost in Hallock. It's got nine hundred people, you know!"

The bus driver retorted, "Hallock's going to pound you guys. I'm just going to drop you off and go home. You'll have to walk back."

The boys, except for the stoic brothers, were amused.

Rod and Chip pulled out flashlights and opened up their

Shakespeare books. Rod recited while Chip prompted him on. "There's blood..." Chip read.

Rod answered smiling, "There's blood upon thy face!" Chip encouragingly replied, "Good." He paused and then prompted again, "He has..."

Rod blurted, "Wisdom that doth guide his valor."

Fred continued to listen to the radio with his head leaning on the windows for maximum reception. Jackie leaned forward and looked at Fred, who had his eyes closed, completely limp with relaxation.

Jackie then slid back and looked at Duane sitting next to him and whispered emphatically, "Fred's hair is frozen to the window."

Duane loudly barked, "Rolle's comin'!"

Fred jumped, startled; his hair, solidly glued to the glass, stayed. Duane and Jackie guffawed heartily. Fred turned to pummel them both when faintly from his radio Elvis boomed out "Heartbreak Hotel."

"Hey, listen! It's a new song!" Jim exclaimed.

The tune faded in and out sporadically. Duane, monkey-like, reached for and grabbed the transistor from Fred. The sound was lost. Fred climbed over his seat and wrestled his radio back and put it snugly against the window again.

Rod recited to Chip, "I have no spur to prick the sides of my intent...intent..."

"But only vaulting ambition..." added Jackie, who had been listening in the seat behind them. He contemplated and then continued in a rare mood of introspection, as he looked out over the vast, inconsequential place outside his window, "...which o'er leaps itself, and falls on th' other."

Jackie closed his eyes and momentarily listened to the pleasant murmur of the engine, rocking its riders ever so gently. Something inside him felt different. He felt older.

* * *

The team tromped into the cramped Hallock coal heater room, which doubled as the locker room.

"Where the hell do we put our stuff?" Cookie looked around in Spartan hauteur and grunted.

"Anywhere you can!" J.C. called out jovially.

The boys found places to set their gear as best they could and dressed standing up, telephone booth style, cussing as heads banged into noses, rear ends bumped and elbows lodged into crotches.

Chip took his new skates out, caressing them before he slid them on, a private gesture no one on the team was aware of except Rod, who looked relieved. The skates were duly rockered to fit Chip's style.

Standing by the coal heater, Rolle watched Chip emotionally. Rolle never told Chip who his benefactor was.

"This is our first test against a team in our region," Rolle told them. "Don't take any stupid penalties. Part of our game has got to be in not making mistakes. We can't afford it." Rolle looked at this odd little group that, for some reason, really seemed to be coming together as a team. "This will be a physical game. Rabe, as you know, is a great player and he has lots of backup from his big guys."

* * *

The crowd was boisterous inside the arena. Hallock was definitely hockey country. Cheerleaders lined the ice as the rowdy spectators yelled their cheers.

The Prowlers knotted around Rolle.

"Watch Rabe. Play tight," he gave as last-minute instructions. The boys nodded eagerly as the buzzer sounded.

Jackie won the face off, as he usually did, skated it down and passed to Chip. Anderson, a huge Hallock defenseman, body checked sinewy Chip. Chip flew in the air spewing, as if the word had been knocked out of him, "Shit."

Dockin, from Hallock, picked up the loose puck with his stick and headed towards Rod. Duane and Fred squared their shoulders and skated backwards while Duane yelled to Fred, "Don't split. Stay with me."

Dockin veered to Fred's side. Fred stayed with Dockin and rode him into the boards behind the net, thus splitting the defense. The Thief River fans cheered Fred, many not realizing the defense had been weakened.

Spritely Rabe swooped adroitly in, scooped the puck out from under Fred's big feet and fired it out to Johnson who, quick as a laser, zapped it into the net right above Rod's shoulder as he went down to save it. The Hallock crowd went nuts. Rod hung his head. He always felt it was his fault if the puck went in and that he had let his teammates down.

It was still the first period and Duane had determined that it was up to him to tie up the game. The big beefy Hallock defense had blasted Chip, Jackie, Glen and Jim Hall into the boards repeatedly; they were getting fried. Cookie and Jimmy had been mashed too, but it didn't affect them.

Duane managed a free puck from the mammoth Sorenson, and skated down ice with it. He could pass to Glen. He didn't.

"Pass the puck!" Rolle yelled from the bench.

Duane continued skating down ice with the puck. Jackie was open.

"*Pass the puck!*" Rolle screamed frantically.

Duane zoomed in on the goalie, shot and scored. Cookie, Jim, Art and Jimmy cheered from the bench. Fred, Chip, Jackie and Glen descended on Duane with whoops of joy.

Rolle stood glowering, then screamed again, "Duane!" then turned to Art. "Cloutier, go in for Glass."

Art looked at him startled but hopped over the boards onto the ice. Duane came in fuming. Rolle was furious. Duane didn't look at him.

"You've got to learn to headman the puck. You do a solo act like that again and you sit out. You hear me?" a crimson Rolle screamed at Duane.

The score remained tied to the end of the first period, but the physical abuse dished out by Hallock was brutal.

In the second period of Hallock's body thrashing, they used their size to every advantage they could, frustrating the Prowlers.

Every time the Prowlers got the puck they were tripped, pushed, flattened or banged into the boards. The referees didn't seem to know what a whistle was for.

The score was stuck 1-1 into the third period. Jim Hall had the puck and a great shot and was just about to score. Sorenson bumped into him, jarring the puck loose. The anger of Thor crossed Jim's face. He had had about enough. He regained his puck, started another try at a shot on goal and this time Johnson interfered. The referee didn't call a penalty, which made Jim boil.

Duane got possession of Jim's loose puck and passed it to Cookie, who had transformed into a raging bull with the abuse of this game. He swung his mighty arm back golf-style, determined to make this shot go in by pure willpower and strength. Instead the puck sailed up, up, up to the rafters, smashed through a window on the high ceiling, launching it into the night. The crowd was delighted.

The vapor was still in Jim's boiling pot. As he watched the flight of the puck, Anderson came by and butted him. The referees had their minds on securing a new puck and didn't see this. Jim bolted away with the power of steam just let out of his kettle. He skated through the crease. Hallock's goalie, Schulte, whacked Jim's legs with his stick as Jim skated through his territory. Jim glared at Schulte and skated defiantly back through the crease. Schulte whacked him again.

The power had been let full out of Jim's teapot. The void screamed inside him. As the other players were lining up for the face off Jim skated away, gliding his tall athletic body around the entire rink, passing behind Rod at full speed. Jim, skating low to the ice, eyes intent, streaked by Rod's side and, as he did, dropped his stick on the ice.

"What are you doing?" Rod hollered as the stick swirled madly around and crashed against the boards.

Jim, grim jawed, didn't answer. He streaked straight down the ice, full speed, temper in full control of his actions.

From the box Rolle picked this scenario up and screamed a full, "Jim, no!" as Jim continued his charge. J.C.'s usually dancing eyes lost their glint and stared. Jim peeled off his gloves, stopped dead in front of Schulte, ice shavings covering him, his precious zone and his net, and in one fluid motion socked Schulte in the face. As Schulte fell Anderson was already punching Jim in the back. Cookie moved in as fast and as dangerous as thick lightning hitting the ground. Rabe, Dockin and Sorenson jumped on him. Cookie got up roaring, shaking them off like flies. Both benches cleared for a melee. The little referees dashed around madly, trying to stop the fights.

In the end Jim was 'thrown' out of the game. He skated feistily ahead of the referee as he was herded off the ice like an errant frisky calf into a pen. He had retrieved his stick and gloves during the aftermath.

A guard escorted Jim back to the heater room where he barged in, slammed the door and smashed his wooden stick against the wall, reducing it to smithereens. Boys' clothes and empty hockey bags were scattered thickly on the floor. An old clock ticked tiredly on the wall.

Jim Hall sat down on the concrete, suddenly very tired.

* * *

The little clock that moved so slowly read 10:05. Jim, still in full dress and still on the floor, heard tromping sounds getting closer. The door opened and the team filed in noisily. They all whacked Jim affectionately as they went by.

"Did we win?" he asked Fred.

"Barely," Fred answered his best friend as he sat down to take off his size twelve skates.

22

baudette

Jackie, his friend Ross, Cookie and Jimmy ambled down the boisterous, crowded corridor at Lincoln High the day after the Hallock game. Mr. Ostby had broadcast the score during the morning announcements, which brought renewed hockey excitement to the school. No one expected to go to State and everyone was keenly aware that Joey was gone, but it was exciting to have won the first two games.

"Good going last night, guys," everyone was saying.

"Thanks," they answered.

A duo of tall thin brunettes passed the boys. Both of the girls giggled and said "Hi." The boys answered "Hi" back. After they passed, one of the girls blushed and said to her gamine friend, "He's dreamy." They turned around and stared briefly at Jackie. He looked back at them in a cocky, teasing manner, all glasses and teeth.

"I wonder why he doesn't ask anyone out?" one of the girls mused.

"I don't know," the other replied. "There isn't a girl in school who wouldn't like to go out with him!"

The boys entered their vo-tech class. Mr. Hanson, a kind, no-nonsense teacher wearing overalls, smiled warmly at them. They approached their designated car and checked their tools methodically. At the other end of the shop a group of boys struggled with an engine, unsuccessfully trying to lift it out with a hoist.

"Mr. Hanson, this thing won't budge," one of the students lamented.

"What's the problem here, boys?" Mr. Hanson moved over to the frustrated group.

"We can't get the engine out," two answered almost in unison.

Cookie and Jimmy eyed each other, put down their tools, and trudged unceremoniously from the car they were working on over to the anxious group. Everyone stepped back when they arrived. Jimmy and Cookie flanked the engine. Without a word they pitched their hands under the motor and lifted it out. The class looked on, stupefied.

"Uh, thanks," the two said in unison.

"Anytime," Cookie answered.

Jimmy and Cookie returned quietly to the vehicle they were

working on and resumed their task, unaware of the stares of their peers.

* * *

Rolle, wearing a checkered bow tie, stepped into the principal's office and skidded dead in his tracks when he saw Jackie alone, sitting in the office foyer, busily writing on a sheet of paper. Rolle nodded stiffly at him and tapped lightly on Ostby's door.

Ostby, hair slicked back and gleaming, breezily welcomed him in, "Dennis, glad to see you!" and closed the door behind them. "I was just going to round you up."

Rolle gulped. "About Jackie?"

Mr. Ostby fluttered a hand of casual dismissal, "Oh, no. Jackie's fine. He was cutting up in history class so I'm helping him do his report here. He's getting into it!"

Rolle folded up into a chair in relief and let out a held-in breath. "Good. That kid lives on the edge." He nervously fingered his bow tie, "I'm a wreck wondering if he'll do something to make himself ineligible."

Mr. Ostby glided behind his desk and tapped the glossy finish with his knuckles, "We're not going to let that happen!" He smiled deliberately and broadly.

Rolle perked up, "Hell's bells that kid's a hockey player. I've never seen such a slick one."

Mr. Ostby sat down in his swivel chair and leaned forward on the desk. "You're doing a fine job with so few boys, Dennis."

Rolle didn't answer. He just beamed.

"But that game today in Baudette..." Kalmer Ostby frowned. "I worry about the boys being outside in this thirty degree below zero weather, Dennis, especially with the wind so strong."

Rolle agreed, "It's terrible, but it's a league game and if we miss it we forfeit it, and I don't think the boys would like that!"

"Well," Mr. Ostby acquiesced, "I agree we can go and we can play, but if it gets too bad, we can always call it off." He smiled brightly, "At least I won my point on taking warm cars instead of that unheated bus!"

* * *

J.C., Rolle, Mr. Ostby, Cy Glass and the Prowler hockey team piled into the men's four cars for the drive north to Baudette. The snow lashed the cars savagely.

Glen, Chip, and Rod cruised in Rolle's car. The mood was upbeat. Rolle and Rod were in the front seat. A smile spread itself across Rolle's face and his eyes twinkled.

"Rod," he said earnestly, "I want you to watch out for the snow snakes. They're sly devils because they're white and blend into the snow. The worst thing is that they can get caught in the net, and they hang there." Rod's eyes were as big as millwheels.

"Just keep an eye out for them," Rolle continued. "You'll be OK."

Glen and Chip spread out in the oversized luxury back seat, looking amused. "But for now," Rolle added, "forget about the snow snakes and learn those Shakespeare lines."

Rod looked uncomfortable.

* * *

The musty Baudette high school gym was a tiny crunched miniature of a real gym. Giggling girls in gym suits played basketball. Their teacher was reffing. The Prowler hockey team dressed for their game under the bleachers.

Duane peered out and teased, "Cookie, that girl is looking at you!"

Cookie looked daggers at Duane. "Shut up," he retorted gruffly.

Duane tried to sound serious, "No, she is! Really!"

Jackie peered out at the girls from behind the slats, "No, she's looking at Art!"

A girl ran toward the bleachers retrieving a ball. Art looked out, "Bless you fair dame! I am not to you known!" The team burst out laughing. The poor girl grabbed the ball and sped back to the safety of her group.

As Glen sat on the floor trying to lace his skates child-style, he moaned, "Doesn't anyone know what a dressing room is anymore?"

"This is crazy," Fred grumbled.

Rolle's head ducked under the bleachers, "It's time, boys."

* * *

The boys trod single file over a heavily snowed-in footpath that led from the Baudette school gym across the football field to the school's outdoor skating rink. Snow pounded the boys mercilessly like a barrel-bodied French woman beating a rug. The shuddering parents waited in the warm, running cars until the game began.

The brutal game was played on bumpy, brownish ice. The wind

sliced their bare faces and stung through their gear. The Prowlers wore several layers of long underwear, except for Jimmy and Cookie, who never donned restricting undergarments and certainly weren't going to now. The storm kerchiefed the rink, and at times Rod saw the opposite goalie as a supernatural veiled hologram moving in and out of sight. Other times he did not see him at all.

Before the end of the first period Glen had possession of the puck and forced his body through the icy blasts. His numb hands managed to pass the puck to Chip who fed it back to Jackie, who dodged a Baudette defenseman trying to block him.

On the bench, which was a dugout in the snow, Rolle, Jim, J.C. and Art, piled over with blankets, stood shivering. Jimmy and Cookie, jacketless and blanketless, leaned over the boards yelling their teammates on.

"Come on Jackie, get it in there!" Jimmy bellowed.

"Shoot, shoot!" Cookie screamed.

The others' teeth were chattering too hard to talk.

Jackie shot hard at the goal. He missed the net, hit the pole and the frozen puck shattered to kingdom come.

A little later, when there was a break in play, Rod was frantically waving and calling to Fred and Duane. They skated obligingly towards him.

"You guys seen any snow snakes?" he asked in an unsettled way.

Fred and Duane looked at each other like Rod was a one-eyed idiot.

"Any *what*?" Duane asked.

"Snow snakes," Rod answered belligerently.

"Never heard of them," Duane replied.

"Yeah," Rod jabbered excitedly. "They hang in the goalie nets!"

Fred and Duane looked askance at Rod and then at each other.

* * *

Just before the end of the period Cookie bulldogged the puck as snow snarled around him. He passed the puck to Jimmy who skated it down rough ice and passed it to Jim Hall, who neatly slapped it in. The goal judge's hand went up like a wooden doll with springs.

* * *

Finally, the faint whistle for the end of the period came through the wind. The mothers had already retreated to the whirring cars and their blowing heaters and thermoses of coffee. The fathers joined them, trying to stamp off the snow before ducking into the igloo-like shelters.

The Baudette team beat a retreat for the school; the Prowlers were relegated to the cozy cedar-smelling warming house. They tramped in, knocking off the snow, and collapsed onto the benches. Trying to unfreeze the ice-packed laces of their skates, they finally managed to get their skates off and rubbed their benumbed feet. Some put them up near the wood burning stove.

"Found any snow snakes yet, Rod?" Rolle, pounding his hands on opposite arms in unison, questioned.

"Not yet," Rod answered innocently.

"Well, keep a watch for them. They grab your skates and you can't move," Rolle chuckled.

Fred had pulled a bench right up to the stove and put his deadened socked feet flat on it. "What the heck's he talkin' about?" he asked Jim.

"Darned if I know," Jim answered.

"I smell something burning," Fred commented, sniffing. "It's awful. I think something died."

The others noticed the peculiar odor but it was Art who hooted, "It's your socks! They're on fire!"

As an embarrassed Fred jumped up, stamping his feet, everyone laughed.

When the hilarity died down Rolle observed, "We've got a 3-1 lead on them. Let's go out and hold it."

* * *

The Poole brood was being served oatmeal. A large stack of toast tottered in the center of the table. Mrs. Poole busily buttered more toast, her back turned away from the counter. Jackie slid two cigarettes out of her pack that sat on the counter top. Pat, Jackie's one-year-younger brother, frowned at Jackie. The radio, a lifeline to the outside world, pulsed a beat behind the family. When it stopped a male voice came on telling the farmers that it would be forty degrees below zero for the next five days. The farmers depended on the news. Jackie ignored it and tossed a few spoonfuls of cereal into his mouth without sitting down. He grabbed a handful of toast, tossed his jacket on and dashed out the door to the hoot of a horn. Chip was picking him up for the early morning scrimmage session.

* * *

A purplish predawn greeted the boys at the windless river. Booms burped from it. It was too cold to talk.

Jackie smoked one of his pilfered cigarettes under the bridge. The silent boys, grim and determined, skated onto the dark ice for their morning scrimmage like waterbugs scurrying for food.

* * *

A cold, maroon-faced hockey team, toting gear, entered the high school punctually a minute before the bell rang. It had been like this for a month now.

"Nice win yesterday!" Casey, a serious but friendly dark-haired boy, praised as they passed. He smiled hopefully, "You guys got a crack at going to State again?"

Chip smiled warmly, appreciatively, as he tugged his gear through the door. "We're trying, Casey, we're trying."

"Well, try hard," another boy added his two cents. "It's my only chance to get to the big city."

The team passed out of the foyer and into the busy hall.

"Wise guy," Jackie quipped.

23

blizzard

Slouched and sprawled behind confining desks in study hall, Jackie, Duane, Art, Rod, Chip and Cookie wore the impatient expressions of boredom. Glen slipped in as the bell rang.

"About time," Duane said flatly.

"Chasin' girls again?" Jackie piped up.

Glen ignored Jackie and turned to Duane, "We still going to the game in Grand Forks tonight?"

Duane fiddled with a pencil, "Yeah."

Cookie butted in, his voice low and raspy, "Who they playin'?"

Duane looked over to him, "University of Minnesota."

Art opened his eyes wide and exclaimed in a high-pitched whisper, "You guys are nuts. There's a blizzard moving in."

He was cut off by the crackling announcements from the loudspeaker carrying Mr. Ostby's chipper, efficient voice. "Your attention for the announcements. The hockey Prowlers play St. Paul Johnson at the arena tomorrow night."

* * *

The liver-lipped basketball coach slouched in his office. He wore his Simon Legree grin as he and his assistant listened to the announcement.

"St. Paul Johnson, last year's state champions, is undefeated..." Mr. Ostby continued.

The coach scratched his hairy neck and leaned back in his green swivel chair. His pale, lithe assistant copied him, the proverbial bad cat.

The basketball coach sunk his teeth into a gooey candy bar and, while savoring the flavor, licked his sticky ringed finger. "Those little punks will get creamed."

* * *

In the study hall the students cheered and the hockey boys sat up, like dogs for a bone, smiling at each other as Mr. Ostby boasted, "...and so are our Prowlers."

Jackie adjusted his glasses and added, with a braggy, too-big-for-his-britches voice, "And they plan to stay that way."

* * *

Friday evening Glen sat on his neatly made bed browsing through *Sport Magazine*. On the wall of his precise, neat room was a tidy bulletin board covered with carefully cut out Prowler clippings and a poster of Rocket Richard. Well-dusted framed family photographs and books lined a wooden bookcase. Outside, a car horn honked loudly twice. Glen sprang up expectantly, looked out the curtained window, picked up his hockey jacket from his bed and hurried out of his room.

He trotted down the stairs and hurried through the well-appointed living room, where his folks and Duane's parents were playing bridge on a card table. Mitch Miller was smiling through his beard on the television screen in the background.

Glen didn't stop but said over his shoulder, "Duane's here!"

His mother looked over her glasses as she arranged her cards, saying, "Where are you going, dear?"

Glen answered as he opened the door, "The hockey game in Grand Forks. The University of Minnesota is playing the University of North Dakota. We're going to see Joey play."

Glen's father trumped a card, pulled his trick toward him, looked up at Glen, startled, and authoritatively said, "No! The weather's going to be bad. I don't want you driving sixty miles away."

Duane's dad eased Glen's dad a bit, "Don't worry, I've already told Duane he can't go."

* * *

Glen opened the car and climbed in. A sizable whoosh of snow blew in as well, partially frosting the dashboard, floor and seat.

Rod, Chip and Duane greeted him, "Hi!"

But Glen cut to the facts, "We going?"

Rod answered, "I can't."

Duane pressingly volunteered, "It's going to be a great game."

Chip combed his hair back with his fingers, "Let's try it, we can always turn back if it gets too bad."

Rod crossed his arms and sat decidedly. "I can't go. My mom said 'no'."

Duane slapped his steering wheel and pressured like an experienced salesman, "Come on! She'll never know."

Rod sat motionless, unswayed. "I can't. Just take me home."

Duane swung the car around and let out one last ditch effort, "OK, but you'll miss a helluva game..."

Rod remained unimpressed. Duane drove one block to Rod's house and dropped him off. After Rod had closed the car door, he turned back and leaned over, motioning Duane to roll down the window. In the background a yelping wind whistled through flawed houses that created an intensity of sound like pressed cries.

Rod looked into Duane's eyes, "You guys be careful. Blizzards aren't anything to fool with." He turned away and walked toward his house, the wind pummeling and propelling him on.

Chip answered, too late to be heard, "Don't worry, we'll be OK."

* * *

Duane drove along the country road on land so perfectly and unnaturally flat that it looked like it was starched and pressed. White stretched taut over everything, an ungainly, uninterrupted sheet. He glanced down at the gas gauge which indicated a quarter tank, and casually said, "We'll have to gas up in Red Lake Falls."

Then the snow started with a mad dance in the wind for a few large flakes. They floated and bing, hit the windshield. Then larger, quicker, heavier flakes came pelting the car.

A few minutes later the car plunged into hard slanted flurries of snow that plastered themselves like bugs to the windshield.

Chip looked forward and squinted through the glass, "It's getting a lot worse."

A powerhouse gasp of wind muscled the side of the car and enveloped it in growing drifts of snow. Storms moved in like walls across the northern prairies. They had all seen them before.

Duane hit the steering wheel and muttered angrily, "Oh, shit. I can't see a thing."

Right then, the car was bludgeoned off the road by a merciless kick from the wind.

Duane, with clenched teeth and an edge to his usually composed voice added, "Holy Christ, we're in the ditch."

Glen looked over, "You got a shovel in the trunk?" Duane nodded, "Uh huh. Two of 'em."

Glen opened the door, wind whipping through his hair and his clothes, as he painfully recalled he had forgotten his hat. "Come on Chip, let's dig it out."

It was pitch dark out except for the car lights. The wind raged and the boys were wind-whipped as they battled to open the trunk, get out the shovels and close the trunk. They shoveled behind the front tires. They shoveled behind the rear tires. Glen forced his way through the wind and pounded on Duane's window. Duane cracked the window.

"OK, rock it!" Glen bellowed.

Glen and Chip pushed the front of the car as Duane rocked it. Finally, in a Herculean effort, the car spun free. Glen and Chip got in, huffing, tossing the shovels into the backseat.

"I'm frozen," Chip shuddered.

"I can't feel my feet. Why didn't we wear our overshoes?" Glen complained.

"Gloves would have been nice, too." Chip rubbed his raw hands together, shivering.

"We have to get turned around and head back. Jesus, I hope we have enough gas," Duane fretted. He peered at the gauge again. It registered an eighth. All three boys looked out the windshield into a solid mass of white.

Duane slid down in his seat, "There's no use to go on. I can't see anything. We'll just wind up in the ditch again."

"Maybe if I get out and run in front of the car you can follow me and we can stay on the road," Glen suggested.

Duane thought about that for a moment, then nodded back heavily, "It's worth a try."

Glen forced the wind-pressed door open and let himself out into the howling night. Duane edged the car ahead following Glen's shadowy form at an excruciatingly slow pace. The windshield wipers worked frantically but barely kept a space clear for him to look through. Duane and Chip rode silently, each with private thoughts.

Finally Chip turned towards Duane, "I think Glen's been out there for about two miles. I'd better take a turn."

Duane sounded the horn and yelled out the window, "Come on in."

The snow did not let up. It got thicker. Duane kept losing Chip behind curtains of the falling snow. He crept along at the slowest imaginable pace. Duane's head was right up against the windshield and yet he could barely make Chip's form out.

After a while Glen intoned, "Your turn, Duane. Chip's been out there a long time. I'll drive."

Duane blared the horn and stopped the car. Chip got in, his face pinched with cold, his fingers nearly lifeless.

Out in the blizzard, so dense it was claustrophobic, Duane took his turn running ahead of the car. He waved his arms directing Glen. The snow only got thicker. The night only got colder. The gas gauge only got emptier.

By the time Duane came back into the car, he was so winded he could hardly talk.

"How far do you think we've come?" he wheezed.

Glen looked down at the odometer, "About six miles, I guess. Let's go as far as we can. It's my turn."

Glen went out again, running through the unbearable cold, having to be practically touching the hood for Duane to see him. He drove until Glen tripped and fell and the car plowed into a snowdrift that barricaded the road.

"Jesus," Duane moaned.

"Glen and I'll try to push it through," Chip responded wearily as he opened the door.

Glen and Chip heaved the car out of the drift. They both jumped back into the car, winded.

"We hit any bigger drifts and we won't be able to get though," Chip said, shaking and out of breath.

Duane inched on, his chin over the wheel and his breath fogging up the glass. He rubbed it absently with his jacket sleeve. His back ached. Glen was outside but he could barely see a foot in front of him. Whomp, they ground into another snowdrift. The car jolted, spasmed, and stopped.

A bushed Glen, breathing unevenly, crawled in, "We can't get through. This drift is packed ice-solid. There's no way."

"Shall we walk for help?" Chip inquired.

"There's no use to try that," Glen answered. "We can't see a thing."

The motor sputtered and died.

"We're out of gas," Duane lamented.

The boys looked terrified.

Chip, dimming with the somber realization, remarked quietly, "Rod was the only one with sense."

Glen dully added, "He hath wisdom that doth guide his valor to act in safety."

"We haven't seen a car for hours," Chip looked glumly down at nothing. "We're going to die out here and let the guys down."

Duane slammed the dashboard, "How could we ever do such a dumb thing?"

The cold boys sat in the cold car and huddled drowsily as the wind spun around them. An hour passed, or two. No one talked, until...

Duane groggily squinted, sat up a little and said, "What's that?"

"What?" Chip murmured.

Duane sat up and looked intently into his frosted rearview mirror. "Something bright in the mirror," he mumbled.

Chip and Glen looked over their shoulders towards the rear window but saw nothing. Glen pushed the door open, while the mean howl of the gale crescendoed in their ears.

He craned his neck, looked behind the car, and shouted, "It's a bus! It's stopped back there!"

They got out of the car, pushing their drained bodies toward the welcome vehicle. A round and jolly driver got out to greet the stranded trio. A shudder ran through his spine reminding him of what could have happened to these boys had his route been canceled. He saw them forlorn and small looking, standing out there against the fearsome backdrop of the night: lonesome road, diving temperature, cavish black sky, miles of nothing, a dead vehicle, snow.

The driver ushered them inside the warm, grumbling bus, "You boys OK?"

Glen, so relieved that he was close to tears, but too numb to cry, answered, "Yeah. But we're glad to see you!"

He swung the door closed and announced to all the passengers, "Hold on, I'm going to ram the bank."

The driver backed up the silver Greyhound and then gassed it, pitching it forward. The passengers lurched in their seats and held on as he accelerated and slammed into the bank. A few crunches of the wheels and a jolt and a bounce and a second bounce and the bus was on the other side. The driver smiled broadly and whistled loudly. The passengers clapped and cheered.

The boys exited the bus at the Thief River Falls bus station. A clock mounted on the otherwise bare wall read 4:25. Chip stared at it, dazed, rubbing his deeply circled eyes, "How're we gonna get home?"

Glen sank onto a wooden bench, sapped of all energy as he answered, "We're not." He stretched out his sore legs. "We'll sleep here. Our parents don't think we went anywhere. They'll think we're spendin' the night at Rod's like we planned."

Duane looked at the hard benches and moaned but he was too tired to think about it very long. Glaring lights buzzed overhead in the dingy station.

"We'd better get to sleep right away, we have a big game tonight," Glen added.

They all looked sick at this thought as they stretched out on the painfully hard benches under fluorescent rods. A lonely train passed by in the desolate distance, sounding a lonely woo-woo against the hardened plains.

* * *

An older man smoking a pipe peered out the windows of the bus station, seeing only gray. He turned and strolled across the shabby room to the sleeping boys, then stood up and kindly shook Chip. "Wake up. You kids can go home now. Storm's lettin' up."

Chip got up, feeling like cold glue, and shook Duane.

Duane rolled over, his hair standing straight out. He looked positively ill as he muttered, "We've got to get my car dug out." He sat up and looked straight ahead at a huge, garishly dressed woman eating a godawful looking jelly doughnut. "I feel like shit," he slurred.

Glen rolled over and clung to his jacket that was serving as a pillow. He looked about as fresh as a pickled pig's foot. "Let's sleep this morning and go back later," he muttered.

Chip was staring at the clock, looking anxious. "We can't tell anyone about this," he said in hushed tones. "We could be suspended from the team for breaking curfew."

* * *

Glen climbed the steps to his porch. Every limb, every muscle, every bone throbbed. He thought about getting past the door, up the stairs and, ahhhhh, to his bed. To stretch out in the clean sheets, in the warm house, and...

As he reached for the doorknob, the door opened. His father, dressed in warm work clothes, was just leaving for the gas station.

"Oh, there you are son," his dad smiled brightly. "Your Mom was just going to round you up. We didn't know if you slept at Rod's or Duane's. I need help at the station today. A lot of people will be socked in." He bellowed over his shoulder. "Stella! Don't bother calling Rod's or Duane's house. Glen's home to help me!"

24

carnage

The Prowlers were dressing for the St. Paul Johnson game. All the players except Duane were in the clean light gray locker room. Rod ground his gum in his usual pregame jitters. Jim and Fred were cheerfully dressing in their corner, exchanging the ordinary chit chat that came with having a best friend.

Cookie and Jimmy were their usual silent, grim and determined selves. There was a rigid sturdiness about them, a maturity past high school and past the glory at hand. They sat on the cutting edge of becoming real men in a real world.

Jackie was ecstatic. "This is our chance, guys! This is what we've been working our asses off all year for!" He banged a locker door, "E-haw!"

Art grinned as he pulled on a sock. Rolle and J.C. were going over some paperwork in the corner. The mood was festive, except for Glen and Chip, who sat on the gray bench looking like the town drunks. No one noticed, probably because each player was so into how well he, himself, would perform.

Glen and Chip hadn't started dressing yet. Chip mustered up a bit of energy to whisper to Glen, "How are your legs from the running?"

"Not good. How're yours?" Glen whispered back thickly.

"Shot."

"You guys dig Duane's car out?"

"Yeah, it was a son of a gun. It was practically buried."

Rolle's voice piped up, "Where's Duane? He's always the first one here."

Jim Hall looked up from taping his knee pads, "His car's out there."

"Oh," Rolle lilted, "I'll go out and see."

Glen and Chip looked at each other and then jumped up like India rubber balls, almost knocking each other down, and spoke in tandem, "We'll go."

"Well, hurry then," Rolle said to them. "You've got to get dressed."

* * *

Duane's '41 DeSoto was parked neatly on the street in front of the arena. Duane was in it, slumped over the wheel, asleep. Glen and Chip ran toward the car, their legs slurred in the effort. Glen opened up the door on the passenger side. "Duane! Wake up!" he yelled.

Duane moaned. His bleary eyes opened and shut like a broken shutter on an old beat-up camera. "Lea' me 'lone," he garbled. Glen and Chip exchanged frantic glances.

Glen shook him, shouting "Duane! Duane!" Duane did not wake up.

Chip bent down, scooped up some snow, pushed past Glen and whacked the snow in Duane's face. Duane woke up like a mad bear. Glen and Chip turned and ran to the safety of the arena, while Duane jumped out of his car in hot pursuit.

* * *

Chip and Glen burst into the locker room, with Duane a step behind. Jackie beamed as Duane, his stalwart defenseman, entered the dressing room.

"Hey, Duane! We'll get 'em tonight!" Jackie grinned.

Duane stood at the door a moment glowering at Chip and Glen, "I'm gonna get 'em alright!"

The comment was lost on the others who were busy with their pregame rituals.

The boys finished dressing and gathered eagerly for Rolle's pregame talk. "As you know, we're facing the defending state champions tonight..." he began, "and they're loaded with talent." Chip, Duane and Glen looked down at their skates.

"They are a clean, hard playing team," Rolle said seriously. "Don't take any cheap penalties. We'll make up for our lack of numbers by outworking 'em."

He looked at J.C., "At the beginning of this season our goal was to win half our games...to be mediocre...not to be an embarrassment." He paused and took a deep breath as he looked at each boy, then continued, "Well, that didn't happen. You have worked hard and won every game we've played this season." His voice rose, "Well, I'll say tonight that you are the best mediocre team I've ever had."

J.C. chuckled. Rod looked like Pooh finding honey at this praise from the coach. Jackie felt pride, Jim and Fred, satisfaction, Art, happy that he was part of this group. Jimmy and Cookie didn't care what Rolle said, and Glen, Duane and Chip felt terribly, terribly guilty.

Rolle paused for effect, then raised his voice in evangelist style and practically sang out, "Let's get out there and play hockey!"

Jackie, Rod, Jim, Fred and Art jumped up raring to go. Cookie and Jimmy got up like they meant business. Glen, Chip and Duane moved themselves from the bench with the energy of salted slugs in a cherished garden.

* * *

The fans were packed in as tightly as rag dolls in a Christmas box. They came to scream and yell and see their Prowlers beat last year's champions.

It was midway through the first period. Somehow Duane, Fred and Rod had thwarted St. Paul Johnson's efforts to score. Glen and Chip hadn't had a shot on goal and a confused Jackie, darting brilliantly all over the confines of the ice, never knew where his wings were. He got glimpses of them back by the blue line or behind the net, or in the oddest places. Jackie had the puck now. He sped down ice with it, flaring his nostrils like Black Beauty. He turned his head to find Glen to pass to him. Glen was not there. Jackie tried a straight shot on goal through the defense, but Johnson's goalie, Tom Wahman, had plenty of time to see it and stopped it easily. Glen and Chip huffed down the ice to catch up to Jackie. The crowd was screaming. Jackie didn't say anything, but he looked angry.

St. Paul Johnson's coach, Rube Gustafson, was talking to his players who were ready to skate out. As one line came in he said softly to the line going out, "OK, 'peanut line', get out there." The sophomore line, David Brooks, Harold Vinnes and Gary Schmalzbauer skated on. Brooks got the puck and started down ice, head down, concentrating on the puck. Glen skated slowly towards him like a lynx cornering a rabbit and stopped quietly in mid ice. He lowered his shoulder and waited for Brooks to collide with him. The unsuspecting Brooks, watching the puck and coming full speed, crashed into the immovable object, a big solid Glen.

Brooks went down in agonizing pain, writhing on the ice. His teammates flocked around him, the crowd became absolutely stilled and Glen stood back, horrified. Chip worked his way over to Glen.

"Christ," is all Glen could say.

Coach Gustafson and Mr. Brooks ran onto the ice and leaned over Brooks as the loudspeaker blasted urgently, "Is there a doctor in the house?"

Tall, thickly built Dr. Greene obligingly made his way through the dense crowd and jumped over the boards to the ice. St. Paul Johnson's two largest defensemen picked the doctor up and skated him out to Brooks, the doctor dangling between them. The players retreated to their benches.

Rolle put a hand on Glen's shoulder, "Looks like a broken collarbone." He spoke to all the team, "They'll get him to the hospital." He looked directly at Glen, "It was a clean hit, Glen. Sometimes these things happen." A sullen Glen looked down the ice for solace, but the ice held none.

The game went on for the disordered little team. Fred and Rod were confused by their always faithful Duane. They couldn't quite put their finger on what was happening but one thing was for sure, Duane's timing was off.

Jackie was vexed and bewildered at his teammates who weren't getting it together. "True, Wahman's a great goalie," he thought as he headed toward the net with the puck, "but we're great forwards...or *were*." His thoughts tangled as six foot four inch Ryan Ostebo mashed him into the boards, bringing him back to his work at hand. The puck was whistled dead.

Jackie won the face off from McKecknie and heard Johnson's coach from the box, "Come on 'big line'!"

Jackie passed to Glen, who was lagging behind. Warren Peterson intercepted it and passed to Howie Peterson, who launched a sharply angled shot from the left side of the goal. Duane lunged but Howie's shot was too fast for him. The puck sailed before him into the net.

Coach Gustafson shouted, "Atta way boys!"

The crowd was blocked out, the fun of playing was absent, but Chip managed a puck to Glen who reflex-actioned it toward the net from twenty-five feet out. The puck was screened and Wahman, mercifully, didn't see it.

"Scoring for Thief River, No. 7 Glen Carlson, assisted by Chip Strand," the voice behind the loudspeaker boomed.

The Thief River crowd went wild. Jackie was relieved. The team rallied around Rolle.

"Way to work, guys. Keep it up," Rolle beamed. He turned towards Chip, "Chipper turn on your speed, get around them." Glen and Chip looked at each other, ashamed.

Rolle's thoughts had already passed to Duane, "Duane, stay on your man." He did his pause-for-effect routine and raised his voice again, "Now let's get out there and score!"

Duane felt helpless, exhausted, spent, worn out and beat. He even sensed a detached disinterest in what Rolle was saying. He tried to shake it off, he tried not to be tired, but if he could curl up on the bench and sleep a few minutes...

The student body stood on the opposite side of the rink from the parents, teachers and townsfolk. Darlene, Cleo, Doots, Karen, Janice, Kay, Ruth and Sandy, junior girls, were by the boards at the blue line. They stood, crunched by all the other teenagers who flocked to the game, but not noticing the uncomfortableness because that was part of hockey and hockey had been part of their lives for as long as they could remember. The girls hung over the low boards, pounding and screaming along with everyone else lucky enough to be in front.

To get a place in front the people came at least two hours early. There was no heat in the arena and it was colder than a refrigerated room where beef carcasses are hung. The combat for cold was layers and layers of warm clothes, long underwear, solid socks, fur-lined boots, scarves, double mittens and warm hats. The crowd helped heat each other, but feet were always the hardest to keep warm.

But when the action was on the ice the cheering section forgot to be cold. Fred passed a long one over to Duane. The puck settled on the ice in front of the girls at the blue line. Duane was lagging at the red line and blonde curly-haired Art Swanson was in hot pursuit of it. Jackie saw this and dashed for the puck, reaching it at the same time Swanson did. They were both the same height and both stopped sideways, hockey style, at exactly the same time. Their blades dug into the ice, sending sprayed ice up over the boards in a shower. The front row girls were bathed in cold white powder. As the girls brushed themselves off, Jackie swung around to retrieve the puck, swinging his stick over the girls. The girls ducked quickly, narrowly missing being whacked in their heads. As they bobbed back up, Swanson grinned at them as he checked Jackie into the boards. The fans ducked again.

Jackie got loose from Swanson, regained control of the puck and passed to Duane, who lost the puck to stocky defenseman Glen Marien. Marien tipped the puck across to Phil Peterson who had just changed up. Phil drilled it hard toward Rod's net. Chip tried to intercept it, but the puck glanced off his stick and flew the wrong direction, into the crowd. It popped off Cleo Hayes' forehead, with only her bangs cushioning the blow, and back to the ice where Chip picked it up. The referee didn't see the infraction. Cleo's friends hovered around the dazed girl, but the play continued. Two hundred and ten pound defenseman Terry Brindley nailed Chip, picked up the puck and sent it to Phil Winter, who skated it in towards Rod as the girls regrouped. Flying pucks, spraying ice, swirling sticks and players' bodies were the hazards of the coveted front row.

The game droned on for Glen, Chip and Duane, who watched the spunky play of their opponents. Johnson's powerful first line, the 'bread and butter line,' scored two goals; Phil Winter flipped a dazzling backhand into the net and twins, Bob and Bill Hult, bagged another. When the final buzzer sounded, Duane, Chip and Glen skated off the ice with the same fog they skated on with. The game was over, the game was lost and the team and the fans had to live with that disappointment.

Whether the Prowlers could have won the game if Chip, Glen and Duane were rested would never be known. The goals scored against them had been brilliant and it was unlikely they would have been different. Jackie, Cookie, Jim and Jimmy were unable to score against Wahman and they all had had plenty of sleep. Tom Wahman was just an awesome goalie and their defense was tight, tough and talented. But guilt-ridden Duane, Chip and Glen blamed themselves.

* * *

Jackie, Glen, Fred, Jim, Rod, Duane, Chip and Art entered the post-game dance dejectedly and stationed themselves at their usual spot by the door. Jim Hall didn't hesitate with them but instead made a bee-line for Janice Helgenset to find solace in her company. They had been a couple since they were freshmen. No one bothered them about it. The Platters wailed "The Great Pretender." Jim and Janice headed for the dance floor. The victorious St. Paul Johnson boys were asking the local girls to dance and the local girls were loving it.

The depressed Prowler team stood miserably at its post.

"Rock Around the Clock" blasted on next, sort of giving everyone a jolt. Angie came over and bravely asked Glen to dance in a hopeful, bubbly manner.

Glen avoided her eyes, "My legs won't take this one."

Another boy walked by and grabbed Angie's hand, "Want to dance, Angie?"

Angie forced a smile. "Sure," she cooed. Angie and the boy danced off.

As the other players looked on approvingly, pain crossed Glen's face.

Jackie, looking like the western horizon of a Kansas storm, growled angrily, "I don't understand it. We don't have a crack at State playing like that."

His friend Ross had found him and joined the group. Jackie turned to Ross, "Come on, Ross. Let's get outta here." Jackie left in a bluster with Ross following.

Fred, who had just played the best game of his life, drifted off and asked Marion Hoagenson to dance. Rod, who had also played an excellent game, Chip, Duane and Glen clustered together.

"Shall we tell Jackie?" Chip asked. "I feel terrible keeping it a secret."

Duane spoke in a deep, controlled, tired voice, "No, we can't tell Jackie."

Glen sighed the sigh reserved for those men who make terrible irrevocable mistakes and pay for it in spades. "We can't tell anyone..."

"Only You" spun off the record player.

Cleo, the girl who got hit with the puck, a young Audrey Hepburn look-alike, stood with her friends in the corner. Darlene and Karen were examining the goose egg on her forehead. A St. Paul Johnson player, captivated by Cleo's beauty, asked her to dance. Another asked fragile, blonde Darlene and Karen's boyfriend, Allen, grabbed Karen. Angie, who was just returning from the dance floor, was intercepted by another boy wearing an all leather red and blue St. Paul Johnson 1955 championship letter jacket.

Glen was watching Angie's activity but continued talking to Chip and Duane, "...but we're never going to do anything stupid to jeopardize the team again." He set his jaw and talked through his teeth, "Damn, all the years we've worked." Glen's voice trailed but he said firmly, "The team comes first from now on."

The floor was loaded with victorious Johnson players dancing with the smiling local high school girls. Angie caught Glen's eye from the dance floor. As they looked at each other she blushed and Glen felt drawn to keep looking at her.

Duane caught the moment. "That includes broads," he said firmly.

Glen sighed resignedly and spoke softly, "That includes *everything.*"

"Let's go home and get some sleep," Chip yawned.

As they left the dance, Glen turned for one more look at Angie.

25

"hurly burly"

- William Shakespeare

In the weeks following the St. Paul Johnson game the boys practiced relentlessly on the gelid river. Their scrimmages were all business, no fooling around. There was only one expression on their wind-slapped faces: intense desire. They skated like "Fantasia," flowing in sync, in harmony. The townspeople, who crossed the river on their way to and from work or on errands, watched them and shook their heads. A pride and solidarity had built within the team and within the town. No one could tell you when it started but everyone knew it was there.

* * *

Examples of intricately diagramed sentences covered the length of a blackboard while Miss Skomedahl explained away. She was a master at this and anything else pertaining to the English language and literature.

"Diagram the twenty sentences on page 201 for tomorrow's homework," Miss Skomedahl announced. Jackie looked at her like she just dealt him a nasty blow with a heavy implement.

He leaned back to Duane, "Do you know anyone who knows how to do this junk?"

Duane looked like she clubbed him too, but had faith in his connections that fed him all the finished homework he wanted. "No, but I'll find someone!"

"You guys should-a-been listening," Glen chided.

Miss Skomedahl, without a breath, moved along briskly, "Let's turn to our Shakespeare lines."

A general groan moved among the students. Art wailed, "O heavy burden!"

The class broke into gales of laughter. Miss Skomedahl chuckled.

She consulted her little black book thoughtfully and looked up. "Ronald Reese," she said in upturned tones.

Cookie, who always looked like a weed in a French palace garden in English class, took a last peek into his book and then closed it. He stared at Miss Skomedahl. His look was as uncommitted to her as it always was to Rolle.

Cookie recited, "Hamlet." Then, taking a deep breath and frowning with concentration, he began, "To be, or not to be, that is the question: Whether 'tis nobler in the mind to suffer the slings and arrows of outrageous fortune or to take arms against a sea of troubles and by opposing them. To die - to sleep - no more; and by a sleep to say we end the heartache, and the thousand natural shocks that flesh is heir to."

The class listened in utter amazement.

* * *

Duane was in the locker room alone, putting Scotch tape on the bottom of Jackie's blades. He hung the skates in Jackie's locker gleefully.

Art walked in. "How do you always manage to get here first, Glabbo?" Art asked accusingly.

"I just got here," Duane responded as he smiled innocently.

The others piled in, banged their lockers open and got their gear organized for practice with Rolle.

"We're winnin' the rest of our games," Jackie gloated. "You bet," Glen agreed.

Jim said to Fred as they started to dress, "I feel like a tough practice today."

Fred grinned, "Well, you can count on that."

* * *

Rod skated out onto the familiar arena ice. Glen and Chip followed, tearing up the ice before practice. Jackie jumped out nimbly. His skates hit the ice and didn't move. Jackie's body lurched forward and then down as he fell flat on his stomach. Duane leaped over him, guffawing, "When you gonna learn to skate, Poole?"

Jackie sat up and swung his feet around. He looked at the bottom of his skates and hollered, "I'll get you for this, Glass!" Jackie peeled off the Scotch tape that Duane attached to his skates as he muttered to himself. He got up and chased Duane around the ice, waving his stick menacingly. They both flew at a dizzying rate in circles around the ice. Rolle's whistle tweaked.

* * *

Miss Skomedahl sat at her desk, "Who would like to recite some lines?" She peered over her glasses predatorily and said, "How about Carlson?" as she looked at her open book. "You have two hundred and twenty five lines so far..."

Jackie stared at Glen from behind and sulked as he watched him smoothly recite, "Double double toil and trouble; fire burn and cauldron bubble. Fillet of a fenny snake, In the cauldron boil and bake; Eye of newt and toe of frog, wool of bat and tongue of dog."

Jackie crossed his arms and pushed out his lower lip, mumbling, "Show off."

Glen mechanically continued with precision and confidence, "Adder's fork and blindworm's sting, lizard's leg and howlet's wing; for a charm of powerful trouble, like a hell broth boil and bubble."

Jackie twirled his pencil and shifted in his seat, looking antsy. Miss Skomedahl assumed that he hadn't learned any more lines and didn't want to be called on. She settled back into her seat comfortably and smiled, "All right, Mr. Poole. I can see you want your turn."

The class thought this was good fun, but Jackie sat back in his chair and grinned at Miss Skomedahl. He stretched out his legs, clasped his hands behind his head and leaned back in his seat. "Macbeth, Act One," he prefaced. Then Jackie continued, "First Witch: When shall we meet again? In thunder, lightning or in rain?" He cleared his throat, swallowed, then continued, with flourish, "Second Witch: When the hurly burly's done, When the battle's lost and won..."

Miss Skomedahl sat up in her chair, amazed and absorbed by the passage and Jackie's strong delivery. She leaned a cheek absently in her soft hand, nodded her head, and took in every word.

26

"marble constant"

- William Shakespeare

Jackie, Chip, Duane and Rod ice fished alone on the snow crusted river. The dark waters flowed silently beneath the ice lid. It was night, but even at night one could feel the sprawling, flat aloneness of the prairie. A fire burned next to them on the ice, casting oblique shadows across their faces. Resplendent northern lights capped the boys.

Chip looked out across the glowing ice that faded into the dark and remarked to the others, "Sometimes it seems like we're all alone in the world."

Rod answered, "Or not part of the rest of the world."

"The fish don't even know we're here," Jackie smiled wryly.

"Winning the state championship we'd be somebody," Duane said, staring at his silent line.

Jackie pulled his line in and rolled over on his back, looking at the blazing sky. "We've just got to win it. *We've just got to win it.*"

* * *

Fred's mother, Mrs. Dablow, sat at her comfortable table in her airy, pretty and very clean kitchen. She had a large scrapbook in front of her, along with newspaper clippings, scissors and a bottle of glue. Coffee steamed from a blue china cup.

She read the captions as she glued, then pressed the articles onto the clean, thick, pulpy pages.

PROWLERS TAKE GRAND FORKS IN SEASON OPENER
HOCKEY PROWLERS TAKE HALLOCK
HOCKEY PROWLERS BEAT BAUDETTE
HOCKEY PROWLERS EDGE ROSEAU
HOCKEY PROWLERS TOP WILLIAMS
PROWLER WINNING STREAK SNAPPED BY JOHNSON 3-1
HOCKEY PROWLERS TRIUMPH AGAIN
HOCKEY PROWLERS WHIP WARROAD

A door banged open as her husband, a train engineer, came in from his run. He looked tired as he walked across the kitchen.

"What have we here?" She smoothed the page as he peered over her shoulder. "Ah, putting the clippings together, I see." He looked thoughtfully and exclaimed, "We didn't think they'd win a game and look at this!"

"I wonder how far they can go," she replied, picking up the next article. "It will kill them if they don't win and yet it seems such an impossible dream they've set up for themselves."

"I know," Mr. Dablow answered as he poured himself a cup of coffee from the percolator. "That Roseau goalie, Olson, was awfully sick when we played them. How that kid ever played with a temperature of one hundred and five I'll never know." He sipped the hot coffee carefully. "He'll be up for the regionals, you can bet on that!"

"I worry about them not getting enough rest and food," she lamented. "They work so hard all the time."

He laughed, "Well, we don't have to worry about Fred eating enough with your three square meals a day!"

* * *

Glen zoomed around the ice on the outdoor rink. He was alone. The temperature had settled so cold it was no use to think about it anymore. His breath, like a jet stream, was behind him as soon as he breathed out. His hockey jacket was snugly snapped and his hat was pulled down over his forehead, with a neat scarf tucked in his jacket at the neck. He had reached a pinnacle of precision, grace and form as he raced down the ice stick handling the puck. Whap! he snapped the puck toward the boards.

Bamb! it hit the bottom rung. Glen swooped in, picked the puck up on his stick, skated to center ice, stopped and sent the puck towards the boards again.

Bamb! The puck hit the second rung and flew back at him. He raced for it, grabbed it with his stick blade, circled the ice and shot at the boards again from about twenty five feet out.

Bamb! it hit the third rung.

The puck bounced off. He smoothly angled it on his stick and expertly smashed it to the fourth board. He got it again, skated the puck down ice, swirled back, shot and hit the fifth board.

Bamb!

As it bounced back at him, he smashed it rebound style.

Bamb! into the sixth board.

He smiled in accomplishment, pulled himself back and drilled the puck smartly down the levels again. Bamb, bamb, bamb, bamb, bamb!

* * *

Rod and Chip finished up a painting job on Chip's car in his garage. They used big, old brushes to lump on a grotesque aqua shade. The newly colored car looked ghastly. Chip stood back after a touch-up, looked at the car, and beamed, "It looks good, doesn't it Rod?" The boys stood next to each other and admired their handiwork.

Rod wiped his forehead, leaving a little trace of aqua across it. "I sure hope we can take Region. I don't know how we'd deal with losing." He knitted his brow and twisted the rag he was holding.

Chip, hands on his hips, answered in an upbeat tone, "We're in great shape. We've worked and practiced and we're a *team*." He smiled, "I always know where Jackie and Glen are even if I can't see them."

Rod wiped his hands with the rag and looked over to him, "Guess we'd better get back to Shakespeare. How many lines we got left?"

"Twenty!" Chip grinned back with energy and zip.

"Well, let's get at 'em, then," Rod said, almost cheerfully.

They sat on the old rug in the cold garage with their Shakespeare spread before them. Chip cleared his throat and began, "Antony and Cleopatra: 'Now from head to foot, I am marble constant'."

Rod beamed, "We are too, aren't we Chip?"

* * *

The invincible team, happy and assured, gathered around a satisfied, confident Rolle who was wearing his Prowler hockey jacket. He looked at each of them as he spoke, "The regular season is history now. We're ready to win this tournament. I'm proud of every one of you."

The boys were quiet, serious. It was their last practice in the arena before the regional playoffs. Rolle had never let up on the drills.

"I don't have to tell you that we're only two games away from the state tournament. Tomorrow we'll take Williams and Friday Roseau. They'll be tough, but we're ready." Rolle gave them a big, unabashed smile and waved them off, "Go home and get a good night's sleep!"

* * *

In the evening the boys scrimmaged on the snow-dusted town rink. Golden illumination from the old pole lights glimmered on the ice. It was their final self-inflicted scrimmage before the regional playoffs. How beautiful, how powerfully they skated as the snow purled down on them. The little boys of the town hung over the boards, awe struck by them. Jackie winked at one as he pulsed by.

The lights snapped off, leaving the boys in the moonlight.

Rod called out, "Think we should call it quits? I can't see the puck."

Rod heard Jackie's voice and saw his dark form as he called out, "Just a few more minutes, Roddy."

27

"sea of troubles"

- William Shakespeare

The sun rose faintly through a light snowfall. Duane exited the back door of his house and walked over to the garage. He had gotten up early and eaten a good breakfast to prepare his body for the game that night. Rolle would have a meeting with the team in the morning, then right after noon the school would have the pepfest. The team would board the bus for the sixty mile ride north to Roseau for the first regional game against Williams. It was a big day and he felt strong and confident.

Duane walked the short distance from the back of the tidy house to the garage. He stooped down, grabbing the handle of the garage door to pull it up. A little skirt of fresh snow cozied at the bottom of the door. As Duane yanked the door it shot up, taking his hand with it while it was still attached to the handle. He heard a loud crack and felt a shock of excruciating pain that riddled his body to the core.

Duane uttered a muffled cry and managed to wrangle his hand free as it sprayed a shower of blood onto the new snow. He stooped and held it with his other hand. A deep. messy laceration exposed the central bone. A jagged piece of it, shiny and white, jutted straight out, completely opposed to where it should have been. Streaks of blood stained the pearly surface.

Duane doubled over in agony and headed back to the house, tourniqueting his injured hand with the other to try to slow the bleeding. His raining hand left a crimson path behind.

* * *

A car pulled up to the City Service gas station, located one block east of Lincoln High. Cookie and Jimmy disembarked on the passenger's side. Their older brother Bernerd, home on leave from the Navy and a dead ringer for Jimmy, got out of the driver's side.

"Thanks for the lift, Bernerd," Jimmy said, almost smiling, as he slammed the door shut.

"Yeah, see you guys later," Bernerd waved a mini salute.

Cookie and Jimmy trudged over the small icy patches one block to the high school. Both were thinking about hockey.

"We'll get by Williams OK tonight," Jimmy offered in his low voice.

"Uh huh," Cookie answered.

"Roseau will be tough."

"We'll take 'em. We have to." Cookie's eyes focused into his thoughts like a predator in the wild eyeing the hole of its prey.

"Then the scouts will see us at State! I know we'll get picked up, Cookie. We're tough and we're damn good."

Cookie had never seen his brother so animated.

"Yeah, we're damn good," Cookie's gruff voice answered.

Bernerd was still in the little white brick gas station talking to the manager. He lit up a cigarette as they chatted.

A dark car drove by. The driver slammed on the brakes and looked into the gas station, then stepped on it and raced off.

Bernerd and the gas station manager looked at each other with question marks on their faces.

"What was that all about?" Bernerd asked. "Damned if I know," the manager smiled, not paying much attention to the incident. "So how's the Navy?"

"Great. I came home to watch my little brothers play hockey."

"Glad you could make it! They're somethin' worth seein' alright."

* * *

Chip, Glen and Rod raced down the corridor to study hall. Their high spirits filled the hall.

A boy passing waved, "Hey you guys! Let's go!"

Casey, walking with him, added cheerily, "Only two more games and this town is in St. Paul!"

* * *

Jackie, Art and Cookie were cramped in their desks in study hall when Glen, Rod and Chip entered.

Jackie looked at them, "Hey you guys, where's Glabbo?"

Rod answered, puzzled, "We haven't seen him."

The bell rang and the loudspeaker crackled as Glen, Rod and Chip sat down. Mr. Ostby's monotone belted out through the room with excitement, "The semi-finals for the regional hockey tournament are in Roseau tonight at Seven. The Prowlers play Williams. Good luck, boys!"

The girl who did Duane's homework turned in her seat and asked

Cookie, "Are you going to win tonight?"

Cookie eyed her, "It's in the bag."

Glen added, "Piece of cake."

* * *

Later in Miss Skomedahl's room, students worked quietly, diagraming sentences. An example was drawn on the chalkboard. Rod, Jackie, Cookie, Art, Glen, and Chip looked apprehensive.

Chip fondled his pencil nervously and whispered over to Jackie, "I wonder where Glabbo is."

Jackie shrugged. "He probably faked sick so he could stay home and sleep."

Rod shook his head and added under his breath very earnestly, "He wouldn't miss the pep rally."

The loudspeaker cackled. Mr. Ostby's voice was terse, "Will the members of the hockey team please report to the gym."

The boys got up slowly, looking at each other, concerned.

As they left the room Chip shook his head slowly and shakily said to Rod, "I didn't like the sound of that."

* * *

Rod, Chip, Glen, Art, Cookie and Jackie tentatively entered the minimumly lit, empty gym. Bleachers that looked like stair steps were pulled out and chairs were set up on the gym floor for the pep rally. Jim and Fred came in.

Cookie glanced around worriedly, "Where's Jimmy?"

Fred echoed softly, "Where's Duane?"

Art jammed his hands in his pockets and looked around the gym, "What's this all about?"

They sat down on the bleachers and waited.

A door creaked at the far end of the room. Rolle's footsteps clicked and moved slowly along the glossy wooden floor. The boys waited, still as posts. Only their eyes moved, all focused on him. As he approached them he just stood for a moment, looking at each one of them through raw, red eyes.

* * *

Outside the main doors to the gym, the basketball coach peered through a sizable crack, spying on Rolle and the boys. His nosy assistant tried to take a peek also. The basketball coach let out a gleeful, vengeful smile, "I finally got 'em."

* * *

Rolle, gaining control and trying to maintain his composure, said in a strangely tight voice, "A couple of things have come up and we need to talk about them."

The boys sat riveted to the benches, hardly able to breathe. All looked panic stricken, even Cookie.

"Jimmy has been suspended from the team for smoking," he continued. "Someone saw him at the City Service station this morning."

Cookie cracked out like a cat-o'-nine-tails, startling the off-guard Rolle. "Jimmy wasn't in the City Service station!" he bellowed. "*Bernerd was!* Bernerd let us out and we walked to school." Anger laced his acrid, booming voice.

All the boys sat stunned.

"Well, let's hope something can be done," Rolle said, trying to bury the pain and hide it forever. "This person swore it was Jimmy and I don't think he will change his word."

* * *

Outside in the hallway the basketball coach smiled darkly in self-satisfaction.

* * *

Inside the gym Cookie lamented, "How could anybody hurt Jimmy? He never hurt nobody." He buried his head in his hands as his neck muscles hardened in anger.

Jim Hall, bewildered, looked shellshocked. "We don't have a line without Jimmy. He's our sparkplug."

"Son of a bitch!" Jackie exploded. "It had to be someone who's jealous of the hockey team."

Rod, looking like Pooh searching for the hefalump, asked forlornly, "Where's Glabbo?"

The boys volleyed their eyes back to Rolle. "And that's the other thing," he said mournfully. "Duane's mother called from the hospital."

The boys looked horrified.

"His hand got mangled in the garage door this morning. One bone is fractured, several others were broken. The hand is severely lacerated."

No one moved. No one even breathed.

* * *

Outside the door, the basketball coaches raised their eyebrows.

* * *

Back inside the gym the boys were dealing with shock.

Jackie injected desperately, "Glabbo will play."

"Yeah," Fred added. "Nothin' could keep Glabbo away."

Glen interjected firmly, "He'll be there."

Rolle said, "Now, now, boys, don't get your hopes up. The doctor might not let him play."

With unflinching certainty, Chip naively tagged in, "Glabbo will play anyway."

* * *

A homespun Mrs. Reese was 'doing up' the breakfast dishes. The room looked more like the late thirties than 1956. The kitchen was clean but cluttered. A crucifix hung dolefully. Bernerd sat reading the paper at the table, smoking a cigarette and drinking a cup of coffee. The door slammed. They looked at each other, surprised. Jimmy appeared at the kitchen door. He stood there, white and shaking. Mrs. Reese's eyes widened in fear. She wiped her hands on her apron as she rushed across the room to her son. "What's wrong, Jimmy?"

"Oh, Ma! The basketball coach told Ostby that I was smokin' at the gas station today. Ma, it wasn't me!" Bernerd's jaw dropped. He set his cigarette down and got up, "That was *me*!"

Jimmy looked from his mother to his brother, "They kicked me off the team!"

* * *

Ross and Jackie took a drive in Ross' spotless, green '49 Chevy after the bleak pepfest.

No one had any pep at the rally and even the band sounded rotten. Rolle looked like he was going to cry through the whole thing and the boys were a positive mess. No one felt like cheering or singing, and lots of kids were crying. Word got around fast about the basketball coach and he made himself scarce.

Jackie and Ross drove alone. They only had a short time before the bus with the players left for Roseau to take the Prowlers to the first regional game against Williams.

Ross rummaged through the glove compartment for his Lucky Strikes as they drove south out of town toward St. Hilaire. Wind filled with snow skipped across the smooth gray road. He offered Jackie a cigarette when he found them.

"I can't smoke anymore, Ross," Jackie said, looking straight ahead at the road. "I expect everyone else to follow the rules...and Jimmy got busted for something he didn't even do!" Jackie sighed to himself as he looked across the bare white level land and said to his friend, flatly, "Jesus, Ross! How can we be in so much trouble?"

williams

the first regional game

Inside the Roseau ice arena locker room Rolle, J.C., Jackie, Glen, Jim, Cookie, Fred, Art and Chip prepared themselves for the game in a gloomy, anxious, and tense atmosphere. Rod sat dejectedly on a bench, fully dressed and focused on an uninteresting crack in the floor. J.C. and Rolle checked over the water bottles.

Without notice the locker room door opened and in barged Duane with a large, fresh bandage wrapped to the bulging point around his hand.

Rod jumped up, stunned. "Glabbo!"

The other players gathered around Duane, while Rod, who would be wagging a tail if he had one, said elatedly, "You here to play?"

Duane stood firmly and looked at him, "Course. Think I'd stay away?"

Rolle came forward and gripped Duane's arm. They looked at each other on the level. Rolle held his head up, fighting back tears.

"We'll be there to back you up if you need a breather," offered Jim.

"Aw, cut it out," Duane answered. "We've got a game to win."

The morale had shot up a thousand percent. Suddenly, Duane looked around, troubled. "Where's Jimmy?"

There was a weighty silence, then Cookie blurted with intense feeling, "He was kicked off the team 'cause someone saw Bernerd smoking and said it was Jimmy."

Duane stared at him, "Christ Almighty. Nobody told me."

J.C. shook his head slowly, "Your parents had no way of knowing."

Jim added, "We're trying to get it straightened out so Jimmy can play tomorrow."

Cookie grimly eyed his line mate Jim, "We have to get by Williams first." Then he looked at the others, "No one can make any more mistakes."

Jackie looked at him and nodded. The quiet giant had become quite vocal.

The boys knotted around Duane, their emotions aroused by renewed commitment, joy and trust.

Rolle left the dressing room and found Duane's father standing in the dimly lit hallway.

Rolle approached him. "Are you sure you want Duane to play?"

Cy Glass turned and faced him. "There was no way to keep him home. He's shot up with novocaine right now, but when it wears off it will be rough. He's got a mess of stitches holding that hand together."

Rolle asked, "How can he hold a stick?"

Cy answered somberly, "We'll have to tape it to his glove."

Rolle sighed, "He'll never let us know about the pain, you know."

Cy took a deep breath and nodded, "I know."

Rolle slipped back inside the locker room. The boys were all dressed and sitting quietly, almost motionlessly. The mood was a whirling mixture of feeling wrath about Jimmy not being there and being sorry about Duane's injury, yet there was an overlay of elation that Duane was there at all.

Rolle paced a bit to collect his thoughts. Then he stopped and looked the boys over, *his* boys over, one by one. He began, "We've been through a lot this year. Today has been terrible. But we can get through this. We'll go out and give it all we have and hope Jimmy's back with us tomorrow."

On the bright Roseau rink in the spacious new arena, Rod warmed up slowly, knocking his pads with his stick and skating alone. Jackie, Glen and Chip loosened up by alternating short bursts of speed with coasting maneuvers. Jim, Fred and Art skated around like lost puppies and Cookie raced around angrily. Back in the locker room, J.C. helped Cy Glass tape Duane's stick to his glove.

Just before the whistle blew Rolle gathered his team together. "The Williams team doesn't know that Duane's hand is numb. We've got to fake it. Just Duane being on the ice is a threat to them. Fred, you'll have to cover any loose pucks back there."

Fred answered him with a no-nonsense nod. Jackie, Glen, Chip, Fred and Duane skated out onto the ice hesitantly, like race horses without shoes headed to the starting gate. Something wasn't right and it affected all of them. They just couldn't shake the way they felt.

Jim, Art and Cookie headed for the bench.

Art was numb with fright. He knew the game, had improved steadily this year and had filled in when the Prowlers were ahead, but this game was so important.

Jim sensed the moment and said, "We've skated together since we were kids. You'll be fine."

Art gulped as he sized up the opposition. Williams' Gillie was a northern legend on skates. He, Bill Charlton, and Speedball Nelson headed for the forward slots. Burly Malcolm McKinnen and Preston Peterson were defense. Wilbur Tviet, an ace goalie, was in the net. Except for Gillie, they were not fancy skaters but they played cold, hard hockey and Art knew that they were there to win.

He glanced across the arena. Fans were jammed in as tight as pickles in a jar. Thief River Falls people were standing by their seats waiting for the puck to drop. Art felt the exhilaration that filled the other players and the fans. He saw all the familiar faces. He couldn't let anyone down.

Gillie snapped the puck out from under Jackie's stick at the face off and skated it down ice like a trout in a clear stream. The crowd was already into the game, yelling. Duane loomed tall above Gillie who tried to skate around Duane, but Duane was on him. Duane's stick hung oddly from his glove. J.C. and Rolle gasped at the sight. Fred bolted over to the rescue, sweeping the puck with his long arms. The puck was jarred loose and Chip was on it, tearing down the ice and passing it up to Jackie, who faked Tviet and shot. The shot hit Tviet's skate. The crowd groaned. Rolle felt nerve bumps lining his stomach.

On the other side of the rink, Williams' coach, McCrady, watched Duane intently. He said to the first player near him in the box, "There's something very wrong with that Glass boy's hand. He can't control his stick."

The period was played hard and fast. Duane didn't let up on body checking or putting his entire body into the game. He couldn't use his hand so he couldn't do anything with the puck. Fred was everywhere, taking up the slack. He had learned from his superior teacher, Duane. At the end of the first period the score read 0-0. Both teams tromped off the ice.

In the locker room Rolle's main concern was Duane. "You going to be able to make it?" he asked.

"Yeah," Duane answered, as stoically as a Sioux initiate.

Rolle talked intensely while he had his chance, "Their goalie's hot tonight but I think he's weaker on low shots. I think Glen should try one of his long, low ones. Jackie, get the puck to Fred on the face off. Fred, pass it to Glen. Glen, drill it in. I think you can get the goal."

Jackie, Glen and Fred nodded. He swatted Rod on the back, "Rod, you're the best. Keep it up, son." He turned to Duane, "Duane, if the pain in your hand is too bad, come off. Cookie will play defense and Jackie, Chip and Glen will double-shift his line."

Rod and Duane looked purely transcendental.

Rolle was fired up, "Let's go out and win this game!" Softly he added, "And then I'll sing "Mammy" on the trip home."

Out on the ice for the second period Jackie won the face off, passed it to Fred who snapped it to Glen, who took aim and launched his accurate long, low shot. Duane and Chip caused a commotion in front of the net, screening it.

The puck zoomed past Tviet, who didn't see it until it settled behind him. Rolle whooped it up with J.C. on the bench, Angie was screaming in the crowd, Glen and Jackie hugged, the perky drummer rolled her drums and the band played the Prowler pep song.

As the boys rallied on the ice Jackie suggested, "Let's hit him again while he's flustered."

Jackie won the face off, got it to Fred who passed to Glen who fired another long one, a little higher (third rung) past the goalie as Chip and Duane again screened the shot.

Rolle tightened his fists, gritted his teeth and did a little dance, the band played, the crowd went wild. Father Noah and his robes jumped up and down and Paul Bedard looked quietly satisfied. The Thief River fans thundered in the background.

* * *

The boys piled onto the bus after winning the game as the driver teased, "You boys sure got lucky tonight!" He sniffed disagreeably, "Whew! That smell gets worse all the time. Don't you guys ever wash your clothes?"

"Nope," Rod retorted. "Bad luck. They ain't been washed since the St. Paul Johnson game and they ain't gonna be." As the bus rolled down the dark highway Rolle took off his hat, held it over his heart and, to the delight of the boys, sang in his rich baritone, "Mammy."

The boys smiled contentedly as the bus rocked deeper through the mysteries and quietude of the outstretched farms, pouring deeper into the night.

29

"foul is fair"

- William Shakespeare

Chip and Glen raced down the crowded hall at Lincoln High as usual. Glen recited as he ducked in and out of people, "Tomorrow and tomorrow and tomorrow, Creeps in the petty paths from day to day..."

Chip's shorter legs kept up with him, dashing alongside, "...'Til the last syllable of recorded time. And all of yesterday's blighted fools..." Glen spun around and then faced Chip, walking backwards as he said, "I hope everyone learned all their lines."

Duane walked past holding an open Shakespeare book right up to his face, muttering, "Double, double, toil and trouble..."

Angie and her constant companion breezed by. Angie looked at the floor, while her girlfriend smiled boldly. Glen saw her and said softly, "Hi, Angie."

"Well, hello, stranger," she answered. And she smiled into his eyes.

Inside Miss Skomedahl's classroom Rod recited to Jackie, "'Tis a sad tale told with sound...with sound and, and..." Jackie pushed him on, "Fury!"

He looked up as Chip, Glen and Duane raced in under the bell, "Hi guys."

Gordon Bredeson, Duane's buddy, asked Duane, "You ready for Roseau tonight?"

Duane lifted his eyebrows and took in a breath. "They'll be tough, Gordon."

Gordon continued, "Can Jimmy Reese play?"

Duane laid his bandaged hand carefully on his desk. "Don't know yet. I sure hope so. We barely got by Roseau with him, and their goalie was playing with the flu that night." Duane looked down at his hand and winced, "I dread facing them without Jimmy."

* * *

The hall was charged with activity as students bustled here and there to change classes. Mrs. Reese, nervously cradling her purse, appeared lost and out of place in her black coat and tightly wrapped head scarf. Her son Bernerd, very much in control of the situation, steered her down the hall.

Mr. Ostby, the basketball coach, Rolle, J.C., and the imposing Mr. Day, the corpulent but very young for his position superintendent of schools, all sat stiffly. Jimmy sat forward on his chair in 'The Thinker' pose in his buffalo-checked wool shirt. The basketball coach, wearing shorts, sneakers and a tee shirt, sat looking spitefully at Rolle, who sat deflated, looking at a picture of George Washington behind the desk. Mr. Ostby answered the rap at the door and nervously wrung his hands as Mrs. Reese and Bernerd entered.

"Yes, yes. Come in," Mr. Ostby greeted.

The Reeses had a knit-in pride that they kept intact by staying physically very close together. Bernerd pulled out a chair for his mother, then he retrieved one for himself and set it right beside her. He motioned Jimmy to move his chair to her other side.

Rolle smiled weakly at them and said, "Thank you for coming, Mrs. Reese." Inwardly he wished these good people weren't there. He wished *he* wasn't there. He knew Kalmer Ostby was having the same charitable feelings.

A kangaroo court would take place. The trial had been determined. Rolle knew it in his bones and the Reeses sensed it in theirs as they walked in.

The superintendent raised his chin and looked down the length of his nose accusingly at Mrs. Reese in an uncaring, brusque manner. "We understand we have a smoking problem here with your son Jimmy. This is a very serious offense."

Mrs. Reese withered into her chair. Bernerd stiffened protectively. The superintendent's snooty attitude toward his mother set Bernerd off. He stood up, put a gentle hand on his mother's shoulder and angrily said, "It wasn't Jimmy, it was me."

The basketball coach glared sadistically at Bernerd, then smiled sickly, licking his upper lip with an 'I've got you' smile. Then, taking his time, he barked at Jimmy, "Have you smoked a cigarette, or part of a cigarette, since hockey season started?"

Jimmy, completely unprepared for this question, turned pimento red and faltered. He looked like a trapped and injured animal. His mother, slumped in her chair, looked at her purse handles as she absently toyed with them. Bernerd stiffened again.

Jimmy looked at the floor, his muscles flexing involuntarily as one long, powerful spasm ran through his body. "Yes," he whispered, choking.

The word sent an invisible charge through the room.

Mrs. Reese looked at Jimmy, her eyes popping out of her head. Rolle, powerless, rolled his eyes back and sighed resignedly. J.C.'s mouth dropped open and he quickly shut it. He felt sick. He wondered about the Fifth Amendment. What a rotten trick.

Mr. Ostby nervously fidgeted with his tie. He knew something was very wrong and he didn't like being a part of it.

The basketball coach sat smugly back, folded his hands across his middle and grinned.

The superintendent glared at the Reeses in a holier-than-thou attitude, then boomed, "You're suspended from school for three weeks and off the hockey team!"

Jimmy bolted out the door.

Mrs. Reese got up in confusion, following him.

Bernerd pulled himself up to his full impressive height, took a deep breath and said quietly and intensely, "Damn you all. You planned this whole goddamn thing and put my mama through hell." He shook his head in disgust, "You bastards."

* * *

The corridor was deserted because everyone was in class. Jimmy ran down it to his locker. He pounded on it relentlessly, sending the message of how he felt to the whole school. One lousy cigarette in his own bedroom at the beginning of the season, before he had become committed. Then he pressed his body against the locker and did something he had never done before. He cried.

30

*"... and now
the fleeting moon"*

- William Shakespeare

There is a somber point in Shakespeare's *Antony and Cleopatra* where Cleopatra realized she had lost her power. "...and now the fleeting moon...", she uttered in desolation. Time rolls down into another time, but the experience of the invincible meeting defeat in any mortal is the same. It is met in the mind, but the mind holds both the poison and the antidote.

* * *

Miss Thora Skomedahl scurried her large frame into the teacher's lounge for a cup of coffee before her next class. The usually busy and alert Dennis Rolle sat with an unread newspaper on his lap, alone in the corner, the picture of defeat.

Thora adjusted her glasses, pushed back her graying hair and gazed at Rolle with the kindness in her eyes of a doting grandmother looking at the grandchild who has fallen off his bicycle.

"Remember the 'fleeting moon,' Dennis," she said softly. "Don't let them be defeated in their minds before they try."

* * *

The winter sun dropped past the snow as the bus, carrying the Prowler hockey team, rolled along the two lane highway north to Roseau, its grand rink, and the final game of the region eight playoffs. Everyone had his own thoughts as the cold bus chugged across the uncommitted prairie.

Cookie sat alone, feeling his brother's void. A deep frustration seethed inside him. He was strong, cold, and remote. Yesterday morning he felt so big, so muscular, so tough, so full of life and winning; today he was reduced to a shell, gutted and left. His glum face trained straight ahead but all his mind's eye saw was Jimmy's anguish.

The pain was beyond repair. Cookie wouldn't even be here, on this bus having anything to do with this stupid school, except he wanted to show them. He would show them all right. He wouldn't allow the bastards who hurt his mother and Jimmy to enjoy the satisfaction of watching the team lose. No way. The Prowlers would win. He'd get as even as he could the best way he knew how. But as the bus moved away from Thief River and closer to Roseau, a little devil danced on his head and prickled fears speared his confidence.

Cookie felt the fleeting moon.

Rod and Duane shared one of the buses' stiff seats.

Rod pulled strength from his teammates. He was fragile and vulnerable, but he knew this and stayed within his circle. His mom would be there tonight. How hard it had been for her since his dad died and they moved to town. He was the last of ten children and she was so proud of him. He had to do well for her and the guys...he couldn't let the guys down. Yet, Roseau's Dickie Johnson was an awesome player. Could he handle Dickie without full help from Duane?

Rod felt the fleeting moon.

Duane wasn't up to any antics this night. His thoughts were clear. He would endure any pain he had to and do anything he had to do for his team to win. But how much could he do with his playing hand immobile? It was useless to him. The team couldn't win without him. He held the hand and cradled it unconsciously.

Duane felt the fleeting moon.

"How is it?" Rod's concerned voice startled Duane.

"It's full of novocaine again so there's no feelin' in it for awhile," Duane answered.

Rod felt uncomfortable. Sweat bathed his spine and there was a cold draft in the bus.

Jackie sat back alone in his seat, eyes closed. All his dreams, all his years of work and all his desire to be better than Joey rode on tonight. He missed the joking, the cockiness, the wildness on the bus. It was the way they hyped themselves up for games. How could they do well if they weren't hyped up? Roseau would be.

Jackie felt the fleeting moon.

Jim and Fred bounced next to each other, looking equally miserable. Jim confided to Fred, "This is the worst I've ever felt before a game." Fred nodded dejectedly. Jim looked out the frosted window, trying to dissolve the lump in his throat, and continued, "My dad wants this even more than I do, I think. I remember how proud he was when he got me my first pair of skates. Now without Jimmy..."

Jim felt the fleeting moon.

Fred bobbed his head again but couldn't answer. He had worked to exhaustion doing what Duane had told him and working on Rolle's drills. He and Duane were inseparable on the ice. Fred knew what to do and he did it. But he relied on Duane. Now the rules had changed. He had to cover for both of them. He didn't think that he could do that.

Fred felt the fleeting moon.

Glen and Chip were paired on the unsympathetic seat behind everyone else, but in front of all the gear that got piled in back. Glen tried to determine how to rise to this occasion, how to help his teammates, but it eluded him. If he were dreaming it would be the kind of dream where you're running through a fog and can't find what you're looking for. Glen had met everything in his life by being prepared for it, by working things out methodically, but this situation was beyond his control.

Glen felt the fleeting moon.

Chip was thinking of the kind person from the town, whom he didn't even know, who had opened their heart to him and given him new skates. He'd supposed Rolle had put the word out but he never knew for sure. That person would probably be there tonight expecting miracles, along with all the other people who had helped the skaters throughout the years: Bedard and Dorn and the other Thieves; the business people who paid for their bus tickets to Eveleth when they were Pee Wees; the people who said kind things to them on the street; the shining, cheering faces in the crowd that he had grown to love; the man who bought their first jerseys on that Pee Wee team; the kids from school; the little town kids who hung over the boards, pounding and yelling them on.

His mother would be there, too. They were alone, he and his mom, so poor. So poor. He planned to go to the army next year and send his checks home to her. Chip wanted to win for the team. He wanted to win for Jackie and Rod and Duane and Glen. He wanted to win for old times' sake. Their dream had been impossible to begin with and now down two...

Chip felt the fleeting moon.

Art quietly mused over the dead silence of his teammates. Sure, these blows were tough. But this silence, this gloom, was what unsettled him most. He knew the others did not think they could win tonight.

Art felt the fleeting moon. And it was cold.

Rolle and J.C. took up the front, sometimes making small talk with the bus driver. Rolle couldn't seem to block out the rage he felt at his own powerlessness. What right did anyone have to do what they did to Jimmy? What sort of person would even want to hurt another person so badly? And Duane's hand. It just felt like everything was unraveling for the team, slipping away.

Rolle knew that the silence wasn't a healthy sign. He knew it meant fear and doubts. Fear and doubts undermine confidence. Lack of confidence lowers self esteem. Low self esteem cuts your heart out and lowers performance. Low performance loses games.

Rolle knew Thora was right. She was wise and had been taking the situation in. He knew her heart wasn't in the hockey as much as it was in the boys getting over this challenge in their lives by giving it all they had. The main hurdle the boys faced tonight was facing that fleeting moon.

Coach Rolle mulled the situation over. The boys were apart from him, this skinny maverick team which was fiercely talented and possessed the most fervent desire he'd ever seen. They were an entity unto themselves. Individually they were so different, but together they formed a whole.

They didn't need a coach tonight. They needed a psychologist and, by gum, that's what they were going to get.

31

"there's blood upon thy face"

- *William Shakespeare*

Inside the Roseau ice arena locker room, the boys sitting on the bench remimded Rolle of a row of chilled mackerel. Rolle appraised them, and, as he had sensed on the bus, knew they were beaten before the start. Duane's hand was taped to his glove. Just looking at it made Rolle's flesh quiver.

Rolle began to speak, his words well chosen before he opened his mouth. "This will be the most important game we play all year. If we win we go to the state tournament next week. If we lose we stay home."

Rolle looked around at the devastated little beaten group who had tuned him off already, but he proceeded. "When Dick Johnson's on the ice I want everyone to play defensively." He paused for effect but it didn't matter. They weren't listening to him anyway.

"Olson's a top-notch goalie. I don't have to tell you that. We'll have to shoot on him a lot."

He let out a significant sigh, "We'll all miss Jimmy." He noticed Cookie's white fists clenching his hockey stick. "It's hard for all of us, but I think you guys have it in you to win regardless of this bad break."

He looked around the team. He knew that the group didn't hear a word he said. He might as well have saved his breath but he went gamely on, softly and fatherly, wrapping it up, "All right, boys. Let's go get 'em."

* * *

Inside the arena the crowd was hushed, tense. The word had gotten out about the Prowlers' plight. The Thief River student body was apprehensive, scared and raging with white hatred for the basketball coach. If they could string him up they would.

The teams huddled around their coaches for last minute words. Coach Almquist from Roseau gave the players instructions. "They're hurting. As a team they're disoriented. Strike while the iron's hot. Dickie, put all your energy into getting a goal right away. It'll destroy what little confidence they have left."

Both teams skated out onto the ice. For Thief River: Jackie, Glen, Chip, Fred, Duane, and Rod. For Roseau: Olson, their goalie, with a badly puck-scarred face, Dickie Johnson, Duane Norman, Dale Thortson, Frank Nystrom and Jim Stordahl.

Jackie won the face off and passed it to Glen, who started down ice and advanced it to Chip, who was thinking about Duane's hand. Johnson dodged in, stole the puck and skated down ice toward Duane.

Rolle looked nervously at this barometer. Chipper would NEVER have lost the puck if he were concentrating on the game.

Duane threw a hip check, which the nimble Johnson dodged. Duane slid and fell. Fred was on the other side, where he should have been, and lumbered in but Johnson's speed beat him.

Rod panicked. Duane was down. Fred wasn't close enough or fast enough to get there. They were falling apart.

Johnson skated in on Rod, one on one, shot and scored.

Rolle watched the scenario. He knew Rod should have had the shot. Rod was over the edge.

The loyal Roseau fans went wild screaming and cheering.

Almquist roared his approval. Rod leaned over and scooped it out, ashamed. Jackie and Glen stood dazed on the ice, looking beaten. Rolle observed this, hating this phantom he had to beat for them. Johnson did a little dance on the ice and whooped it up with his teammates.

Deep in the guts of the crowd, the Reeses, the Pooles, the Carlsons, the Glasses, Rod's and Chip's mothers, the Halls, the Dablows and all the Prowler families had been dealt a blow. Bedard and Father Noah stood next to each other, obviously upset. Only Glen's mother spoke, an anxious, meaningful, "Oh...dear."

On the ice again, Johnson stole the puck on a pass from Jim to Cookie. He darted by Duane just as Duane jumped at him, missed, and landed flat on his stomach. Johnson whizzed by Duane like roadrunner, 'beep, beep.' Duane lay on the ice for a second trying to get a handle on the pain. He got up on his knees just in time to see Johnson faking out Rod and scoring.

Art, Cookie and Jim appeared to be washed up, whipped. Cookie's teeth were clenched hard, to keep him from shaking, from losing control. All around the Roseau crowd cheered loudly, their chanting pressing in on the pain. The entire Thief River cheering section was on the verge of tears. Rolle turned away, sick. Rod just stood alone, lost and sad.

The clock on the far wall read:

Home 2 Visitor 0 Period 1

"Five, four, three, two, one!" the Roseau section chanted. BUZZZZZ went the signal for the end of the first period.

* * *

Inside the locker room the Prowlers sat gloomily on the benches. No one talked. The clock read 8:43.

* * *

Everyone just stared into space and looked miserable. As they mutely sat, they heard Roseau's Coach Almquist's voice booming from the adjoining locker room, "We've got 'em! They're beaten inside and that's what counts." Another voice shouted back, "Let's keep it up! Let's pulverize them!"

The Prowlers continued to sit, to stare. The only sound in the room now was the clock ticking. It read 8:53. Rolle had not come in to give them a pep talk. Again, Coach Almquist was heard through the walls, "Keep 'em running. They're disoriented."

Rolle stood in the hall with J.C. "I've got to think of something to move them." He was thinking with his brow pulled tight. "They've beaten themselves."

"Good luck, Dennis. It will take a miracle to turn them around," J.C. observed honestly.

"I just might have something," Rolle answered encouragingly. "It's worth a try."

Rolle took the few steps down the hall to the locker room, opened the locker room door, but did not go in. Rolle looked quietly in the room at the suffering boys, leaned in a little and spoke poignantly, "You guys can't skate." Then as quietly as he appeared, he left, shutting the door firmly.

Coach Almquist's voice got louder and louder, as the Thief River Falls team soaked in what Rolle said. Almquist was all pumped up, "Let's get out there and skate them under the ice!"

Chip miserably kicked a wall, "I wish he'd shut up over there."

Jackie sat up and leaned forward. His voice broke when he began to speak, "Rolle's right. We're a bunch of wimps." A light went on in his head, comic book style. "We're not trying hard enough..." He almost smiled, "Let's try what we did to Williams."

Glen perked up a bit and the rest showed signs of interest. He nodded, "Yeah."

Jackie grabbed his hockey stick, "OK, Fred?"

Fred stood up, "I'm ready."

Duane added grimly, "I'll tie up Dickie Johnson. He won't get by me. I'll get him this time whatever it takes."

Cookie said nothing at all. He had to get a goal for Jimmy. He had to do his part.

* * *

Jackie looked intently at Glen as they skated onto the ice. The old feeling was creeping back. Glen nodded to him slightly as he had a thousand times in the past. Jackie stole the face off from Johnson like his life depended on it and fired it, long and hard, to Fred, as Duane aimed and smashed Dickie Johnson. Fred drilled it to Glen, who shot the puck very long and very low and very accurately. Glen's perfectly executed shot arrowed past Roseau's goalie and into the net.

Jackie and Glen embraced and shouted. Rolle jumped up from his bench, waving his hat. The Thief River fans jumped wildly up and down. The Thief River families screamed and screamed. Bedard shifted feet as he felt the boys getting it back together.

Jackie pleaded emotionally on the ice with Glen and Chip, "I want one more. Christ Almighty, we've come this far." He had to yell over the roar of the crowd even though Glen and Chip were right there with him, "*We've got to go to State!*"

Jackie took the puck at face off. Chip and Glen flanked him as he skated down ice. They were now the masters. He faked a pass to Glen, drew out Olson and whipped the puck by him and into the net. The Poole family went bananas as the band blared under the roar of the crowd.

* * *

As the teams skated off the ice after the second period, the clock told part of the story:

Home 2 Visitor 2 Period 2

The other part was that, inside, the Prowlers knew they could win.

* * *

There was happy bedlam in the locker room.

Rolle joyfully praised the noisy little group, "That's the way, boys. Now you're playin' hockey!"

Cookie fervently declared, "Ain't nothin' goin' to stop us. No damn liar, nothin'." He emptied a Coke and slammed the bottle into the waste basket. "I promised Jimmy a goal. Next one's mine, guys."

Rolle eyed him compassionately and then quickly clapped his hands, "Let's go!"

* * *

The boys skated on to the wild crowd's roar. Action was tense. And then, in the heat of play, Duane pressed Stordahl into the boards. Stordahl kicked the puck out. Nystrom swirled in, picked it up and passed it back to Johnson as Fred checked him. Rod, intent on stopping the puck, moved up ice anxiously, too far out of the net. Cookie raced in to help.

The crowd was shouting to Rod, "Get back, get back!"

Johnson angled a powerful long shot toward the net.

Rod saw the puck coming straight behind him, fast as a bullet. He looked caught, frantic, and coasted on his skates backwards to get back to the net. The fans screamed. Cookie was almost between the puck and Rod; he lunged to block the puck. It hit him square in the face. His huge body sank to the ground, blood spurting from the wound onto the gray-white ice.

Duane, Art, Fred, Rod and Jim raced up to him. Rolle ran out onto the ice.

Jackie craned his head from the bench. "Jesus," he exclaimed to Glen and Chip. Glen and Chip were speechless.

Cookie's blood-soaked face was cut open in a nasty jag under his eye. The boys, Rolle and J.C. helped him off the ice to the bench. Cookie was under his own power but dazed from the hit.

From the stands the Reese family looked on, undisturbed. "He'll be OK," his dad gruffly said to the other parents. "Just a little cut. Nothin' to stop a Reese." The other parents eyed each other but didn't say anything.

Rolle sat Cookie on the bench. J.C. handed Rolle a compress, which he held on the wound. "It's a nasty cut, Cookie. It's going to need a lot of stitches. I'll put a bandage on it for now and we'll get you to the hospital."

The crowd was screaming "Two, four, six, eight, who do we appreciate? Cook-ie! Cook-ie! Cook-ie!"

The team hovered behind Cookie as Rolle bandaged him. The referee skated over and said tersely, bordering on nasty, "We've got to get on with the game."

Rolle, still bandaging Cookie, bellowed, "Chip, take Cookie's wing."

"No!" demanded Cookie urgently. "I've gotta go back on."

Rolle's and Cookie's eyes met. It was the first time they had looked at each other with empathy. Rolle hesitated. Then, realizing the importance of the moment for Cookie, he lowered his voice, "OK, son. You can finish your shift." Cookie skated out to the roar of the crowd with a puffed, quickly swelling shut eye, blood dripping down from under the bandage. Art, Jim, Rod and Fred swatted him on the rear with their sticks. A look of mutual understanding came his way from Duane.

"That's my boy," Mr. Reese beamed.

The clock read:

Home 2 Visitor 2 Period 3 Time 2:58

On the ice and into the action, Art had the puck. He had shelved his fear and skated it resolutely in toward the net. He dodged an off-balance Nystrom and snapped the puck smartly to Jim.

"Atta way, Art!" Chip beamed encouragement from the bench.

Jim Hall took the pass from Art and skated down with Norman hovering over him. Norman skated backwards, blocking Jim.

Cookie's jaw was set. Jim was able to get the pass off to Cookie. Cookie saw his chance. He grabbed the puck with the blade of his stick and aimed at the nets; he was seeing double because of his injury. With all his tremendous strength, Cookie drove the puck toward the goal. The puck flew past Olson as fast as an uncharted comet.

In ecstasy Cookie turned his bulk down the ice, flashing his skates as fast as they would go, waving his stick in the air. Globulated blood pressed out from underneath the bandage. He stopped dead at center ice, shavings flying, pulled himself up to full height, his stick extended straight up in the air.

Cookie stood in triumph, shouting up to the crowd, "That's for you, Jimmy!"

Rugged Jimmy stood up, eyes brimming with tears, as the entire Reese clan waved back.

The Thief River crowd went wild with a screaming, standing ovation that would have been the envy of any rock star anywhere.

Rolle hung over the boards going wild, waving his newly "feathered" fedora cap to and fro. Rod banged his stick noisily on the ice. Jackie, Chip and Glen celebrated on the bench. The Thief River crowd was in ecstasy. Janice, Jim's girlfriend, cried from happiness. She knew that assist was the most important of Jim's career.

At the end of the game the clock read, in the favor of the Prowlers:

Home 2 Visitor 3 Period 3

* * *

The trip home was delayed for an unscheduled stop at the Roseau hospital, where Cookie was stitched up. The snow turned into a blizzard, and the road turned to sheets of ice. Then the victory bus moved south to home through the snowy night as a caravan of happy Thief River Falls fans, who had patiently waited with the bus, followed them in their cars. It was a blizzard icy night. The procession home was slow. Cars skidded off the road, but always the passengers of the next car pushed the stuck cars onto the road again.

It was dark inside the old bus. How strange that it could have seemed cold on the trip up. Now it seemed warm and pleasant. A look of satisfaction and contentment played on the faces of the boys, J.C., and Rolle as he sang, in his ever beautiful baritone, "Mammy."

32

"kindred spirits"

- William Shakespeare

"Ain't that a Shame," by Fats Domino, blared across the city auditorium as the high school students danced their legs away. It was an 'up' night. The hockey players were surrounded by well wishers at their usual knot by the door.

The following Wednesday they would leave for St. Paul and the 1956 State High School Hockey Tournament. The song ended and a loudspeaker took its place. "The next song is ladies' choice." The soft music of "Moments to Remember" followed the loud voice. Girls started pulling boys onto the dance floor.

Jackie mumbled nervously to Ross, "Let's get outta here for awhile, Ross, I don't feel like dancing."

"Sure," Ross answered.

Too late. Two shyly smiling brunettes were upon them. Jackie and Ross looked hesitatingly at each other, then followed the girls to the dance floor.

Angie started haltingly toward Glen and stopped. He caught her eye and smiled at her. They walked toward each other and wove onto the floor, losing themselves in a sea of dancers. Jackie looked uncomfortable and stiff as he danced with the smiling girl.

* * *

After the dance the group migrated to Kife's, a teen dive on the edge of town. Elvis' hit, "I Was the One," blasted through a jukebox and wafted through the door. Kife's was noisy and packed with happy teenagers. Joey and Barbara were there also, home from college for the weekend.

Casey walked by the players, who were all present except Cookie. They were scrunched in a huge booth at the very back of the restaurant and had pulled up chairs for the overflow. Gordon was there with Doots, the drummer. She was quiet and neat to perfection. Casey asked, after sipping on a Coke he was holding, "You guys gonna win State?"

They became quiet. Jackie and Glen looked at each other.

Duane's friend, Gordon, answered firmly, "You bet they are. Doots wants to roll the drums when they skate out under the lights!"

"Yeah, you guys," she said teasingly, batting her lashes that protected huge blue eyes, "I want my drum solo."

The kids laughed.

Casey continued on a serious note after the gaiety had died down, "Did you know that Jimmy is going to Alaska?"

There was a shocked silence but Rod stared back and said, "No!"

"Yeah, he has an uncle up there." Casey's serious brown eyes betrayed sadness, "He's not finishing school."

Duane slid his empty sundae dish away and slumped over. "That bastard really screwed up Jimmy's life, didn't he?"

Jackie contemplatively remarked, "We'll never get to skate together again."

Everyone looked glum.

Chip slurped the last of a tall chocolate shake and said, "You comin' to State, Joey?"

After swallowing a mouthful of chili, Joey answered, "I can't, but I hear the championship game is going to be televised."

Glen looked at Joey in disbelief, "I never heard such a thing!"

"Well, that's what I heard."

"Can you get it all the way in North Dakota?" Rod put in, equally amazed.

"I guess so."

Gordon chewed on a heavily salted french fry ladened with catsup, "You guys looked great in Roseau," he said.

Joey sat back, put his arm around Barbara and focused on Duane's bandaged hand. "Just don't let anything more happen to any of you."

* * *

With Joey home for the weekend, the Poole boys shared a bedroom again. It was nice having Joey back. The brothers talked about hockey until sunup, sharing their independent ice experiences since they had last seen each other. Joey's team at the University of North Dakota had been strong and they were going to play Colorado College the following week in the college playoffs.

"I'm proud of you, brother," Joey said. "You've done a great job with your team."

The rivalry had vanished and was replaced by mutual respect.

"You'll get All State," Joey continued, "...and think how proud

Dad will be with *two* All Staters!"

Jackie felt a lump in his throat so big he couldn't answer.

* * *

St. Bernard's Catholic Church was filled for mass. Ave Maria was being sung by the congregation as altar boys carried the cross and candles down the aisle. They were followed by Father Noah, who smiled at his parishioners along his short journey. The priest stopped at Jackie, his eyes proud. He grabbed Jackie by the scruff of the neck affectionately, "You can win, you know." Jackie smiled back as he and the priest bear-hugged firmly, as if the priest was a favorite old uncle.

* * *

Because of what the boys had been through, the sendoff pepfest for the 1956 hockey team promised to be a humdinger. The Lincoln High School gym was crammed. Chairs lined the entire gym floor so as many people as possible could join in. Mr. Ostby, Rolle, J.C. and the team were cramped up against the wall under the basketball hoop in a row of chairs. Rod and Jackie, the co-captains, sat front and center. There was an empty chair next to Cookie in honor of Jimmy.

The cheerleaders had a small space to lead their cheers.

The crowd wasn't there so much to cheer the team on to victory, as they were the previous year; now it was more to honor the boys for what they had accomplished against adversity, and to wish them well.

Remembering the intense heat in the gym from last year, the boys left their jackets in their lockers and wore cotton shirts.

Paul Bedard was there, Father Noah, the families and just about everyone the boys had known throughout the years. Mr. Hanson, the shop teacher, sat next to Thora Skomedahl.

"I guess the boys all memorized their Shakespeare," Mr. Hanson ventured.

"They sure did. Every one of them," Miss Skomedahl beamed.

Mr. Hanson gazed down at the team. "They're really something, these boys." Cookie's eye was black and swollen shut. A large white bandage was taped under it by the medical team to cover the twelve stitches. He looked more like a heavyweight fighter than a schoolboy. Duane's hand was freshly wrapped and resting on his lap. The entire team looked peaceful, he thought. Self-assured.

The subdued team had humbled from a year ago and the crowd felt it. Rolle walked up to the mike and raised a hand. The adoring crowd quieted.

Rolle began, "We have before us a very special group of boys..."

The crowd started roaring.

Rolle held his hand up again, "...who overcame a great deal of adversity to become the Region 8 Champions."

The crowd roared again. Rolle waited.

He looked over at the boys and then back up at the crowd and put his hand up yet again, "I know these boys will put out to the maximum," he added, "because that is what these boys are all about." Then, huskily he boomed, "And now, let's hear it for our 1956 Prowler hockey team!"

Doots rolled the drums as Rolle motioned the team up to the mike. As the boys moved up shyly, the deafening thunder of fans told them how much they were loved by the entire town. Rod and Jackie moved up to the mike. The crowd quieted in expectation. Before Rolle stepped away from the mike he announced, "And now, our co-captains!"

The crowd cried out, then quieted in respect as Jackie raised his arm.

Jackie took a moment to look into the crowd. He saw eager, supportive faces riveted on him. Appealingly he spoke, "We want you to know how much we appreciate your support...especially after the last two games."

Blotchy-faced but composed Rod leaned toward the mike for his turn, "Knowing you've been behind us has been great for us. Thank you."

The crowd burst into absolute pandemonium. The drums rolled as the band picked up the fight song, and the cheerleaders sang and jumped as the team watched from behind the mike.

* * *

After the pepfest, Rolle and J.C. closed the door to the tiny athletic office. The bus was running and gear was being packed into it. The parents and many townsfolk would follow the bus with their cars. The weather was cold and very windy, so it was a good idea to caravan in case anyone had car trouble.

Rolle looked at kindly J.C., "Thanks for helping us, J.C. I don't know what we would have done without you this year."

J.C.'s eyes brightened as he responded, "I've enjoyed every minute of it, Dennis."

"Last year we thought we had it in the bag," Rolle reflected sadly. "We had it all." He took his heavy overcoat off the rack and put it on as he said, "This year we have this scraggly group, we will probably be on the bottom of the favored list and I think *they* think we can win it."

"With a little luck, who knows?" J.C. answered.

"We'll be up against powerhouse teams but I don't have the heart to tell them. Let's let them enjoy the Roseau win for a couple days." He hesitated as his thoughts switched tracks, "You got the food vouchers?"

J.C. patted his coat pocket, "Right here. Ostby gave them to me before the pepfest."

"Good. The whites are packed. I made sure of that!" Rolle looked happy, "At least that's one problem we won't have!"

As they left the cozy little office and shut the door, Rolle smiled a contented smile, "I guess we're ready, then."

33

edina

It was warm-up time for the first game of the 1956 tournament. The Prowlers skated out in style this year, wearing snazzy new white jerseys with "PROWLERS" spelled formidably across the front; last year and the eleven overtimes were but a hazy memory. Cameras flashed and the bellowing crowd was deafening. Cheerleaders dotted the ice. Droves of Thief River Falls people, city people, and people from the other teams that were participating filled the arena seats. One area was predominantly green, representing Edina, the prosperous Minneapolis suburb.

Inside the announcer's box, Doug Teigmeier, hyped up and eyes glued to the rink, talked into the big mike on his desk, "Ladies and Gentlemen, welcome to the 1956 Minnesota High School Hockey Tournament. Thief River Falls is taking on Edina in their first game. Jack Poole, the Prowler superstar, and Larry Johnson, the pride of the Edina Hornets, two spectacular..."

Way down below, Rolle waved the boys off the ice from where he and J.C. patrolled the box. Rolle looked sharp, sporting a new bow tie, his hat fashionably cocked.

Jackie leaned against the boards, his face flushed. He took slow, deep breaths. Glen's calculating mind was winding up, his muscles twitching like a cougar waiting to strike. Cookie and Jim, still reeling from Jimmy's loss, looked like invincible cast iron kettles. Art huddled close to them.

Rolle started, "OK, boys. We're ready." He spoke in low, terse tones. "Don't let them intimidate you. Larry Johnson's going to want this win. He's a winner, powerful and tough. He has speed, drive, and stamina, and is used to getting his own way. And he has strong players to back him up. But don't forget what *we've* gone through to get here."

Duane and Jackie looked at each other, those two boys who never really knew each other off ice, but whose minds were cloned on ice.

"Everyone's got to give extra to make up for Jimmy." Rolle sighed like Yoda. "Three more wins to the championship."

Rod, Duane, Fred, Jackie, Glen, and Chip skated out to the mighty roar of their fans. For Edina it was Larry Johnson, Bill Strout,

Leroy Ryan, Roger McVeety and Fred Ashenbrenner, all boys from wealthy, privileged, upper-class homes and families. They were used to winning. The formidable Murray MacPherson took his net. Rod, feeling like an old-timer, took to his net, chewing his gum on fast forward.

Self-assured Ryan barked to Larry Johnson and Strout, "Let's get one right away, Larry!" Johnson grinned, "Sure, Leroy."

Larry Johnson won the face off and snapped it to Ryan, who caught it and started down the smooth, moist ice. Duane and Fred skated backwards and Fred rode Ryan into the boards. Jackie swooped in, picked up the puck and passed toward Chip. McVeety intercepted it and drilled it to Johnson, who fired a sure, clear backhand. Rod stilled like a deer facing headlights, and "Zip", the puck flew past him into his net.

The green crowd, laced with svelte, mink-coated women, went wild. Jackie, Chip and Glen looked like chickens viewing the fox who had just gotten into their den. Rod whisked the puck out angrily. Over the loudspeaker a voice announced, "Scoring for Edina, Larry Johnson, No. 7."

As the lines changed, Rolle entreated, "Don't let it throw you. Get out there and show your stuff!"

The boys nodded eagerly.

Throughout the period the ice action built. Chip shot a dazzler, but MacPherson stopped it nonchalantly as the crowd gasped. Jackie shot, Glen shot, Cookie shot, Jim shot. Every trick in their bag was thwarted handily by MacPherson, who didn't seem to know he was being tricked.

"That MacPherson kid's hot. They can't buy a goal," Rolle said to J.C. as he nervously adjusted a tie that seemed to be choking him.

On the other end of things, Rod did the same, stopping every shot that Johnson and his posse gave him. At the end of the period the score remained with Edina at 1 and Thief River Falls 0.

A tense mood settled in the locker room as the Prowler team gathered. "You guys have got to start cutting loose more. We need more shots on goal. Shoot low and go for the rebounds," Rolle instructed.

Duane's face was contorted in pain. Fred was getting used to it, but leaned over and murmured, "How's that hand, Glabbo? You're taking quite a beating from Johnson."

Duane shrugged that off, but frustration edged his voice, "The bandage is a son of a bitch. I can't control the puck." Duane pulled his hand out of the glove. Globs of matted blood oozed out of the bandage.

Rod looked and gasped, "*It's bleeding!*"

Fred and Duane looked toward Rolle and J.C., who were busy talking.

Duane looked back at Rod, "Shhh. Don't let Rolle or J.C. hear you." Duane stuffed his offending hand back into the glove.

Jackie set his hand on Duane's shoulder. A choking at-one-ness could be felt among the players as they all looked at Duane.

Jackie whispered huskily, "Hang in there, Glabbo. We're so close now..."

He couldn't go on and Duane couldn't look at him, but he sort of kicked his skated foot up and put it down again, which was as good as a nod to Jackie.

"I can almost taste it," Jackie continued.

Chip took a deep breath and shut his eyes, "We've wanted to skate out under those lights of the championship game since we were kids."

"MacPherson's got to have a mistake in him," Glen reflected thoughtfully. "We'll just keep pelting him."

* * *

Teigmeier lit his Camel and started up his one-sided conversation with the mike, "The second period is about to begin. It's a tight game. Edina leads one to nothing."

The period was wild. Both teams fought for their hockey lives. But there were no goals on either side.

Then Jackie got a breakaway. He blazed down the ice with the puck, confident of himself and his skills. Johnson and Steinweg both targeted him and aimed to stop him. They rushed in on him fast and strong, smashing him into the boards.

Jackie felt a searing pain as he gripped his wrist.

Chip zoomed up to him, concerned. "You OK, Jackie?"

Jackie gritted his teeth, "It's my wrist."

The house announcer read over the loudspeaker, "Penalty on Edina, No. 4, Robert Steinweg, two minutes, boarding." Steinweg skated off to the penalty box. Johnson swatted him with his stick as he went.

Rolle looked anxiously at Jackie, who was doubled over, still holding his wrist.

After the face off there was a mad scramble for the puck at the blue line. Johnson got it and passed to his wing, Ryan. Jackie intercepted it as Ashenbrenner tripped him. The referee didn't see, or chose not to. Jackie, lying on the ice, saw Johnson about to skate by him near his feet. Smiling, he thrust his foot out behind himself, tripping Johnson. As Johnson fell, Jackie looked at him, with an expression on his face to let Johnson know that he wasn't getting away with anything. In the scramble, and flat on the ice, Jackie managed to tip the puck to Chip, who quickly passed it to Glen. Glen skated it down and passed it back to Chip, who drilled a hard shot toward the net and past MacPherson.

In the announcer's box Teigmeier grabbed the mike and yelled excitedly, "Strand scores! We have a tie game!" Then Teigmeier leaned over his desk and screwed up his eyes, focusing on Jackie on the ice. Apprehensively he added, "It looks like Poole's in a lot of pain. He's holding his wrist again."

Throughout the noise-splashed arena the Thief River Falls crowd jumped and screamed festively. The little band pumped out the fight song.

The score, at the end of the second period, was 1-1.

* * *

On ice during the third period both teams were still hot, but that included the goalies. It was increasingly hard for Jackie to control the puck; his wrist was throbbing and swelling. He watched in pain as Johnson zipped in, intercepted a pass to Chip, and started skating purposefully toward Rod. He watched in pain as Duane lunged at Johnson, just as Johnson drilled a hard backhand shot toward Rod. Rod poised to catch it baseball-style, and missed.

The Edina fans screamed again and their huge band picked up their fight song. It seemed as if the entire place was green.

The Thief River parents were edgy. The boys had come so far and the parents had quietly understood their desire and had witnessed the dedicated grind their sons had put themselves through. Surely it couldn't end as inauspiciously as this.

It was almost the end of the game. The Thief River people were feeling the fleeting moon. The boys had worked hard, but the cards stacked against them were just too many.

Rolle hadn't given up. He gathered Glen, Chip and Jackie around him, "We've got to forecheck harder. Put more pressure on them. We've got to score...and soon." He looked daggers at Duane and Fred and said severely, "You've got to hold them."

Jackie wondered just how much more he could put out. His wrist hurt as if it were being screwed into a vice. He looked over at Duane, who was in another world, thinking about something. "He's psyching himself up," Jackie realized. "If Duane can play in all that pain for this many games, I've got to do more. I can't let the guys down. It's up to me. Get a grip..." His thoughts ran on top of each other, hurdling out of control, thundering in his brain.

The whistle blew, the puck was dropped. Jackie forgot his cluttered thoughts. He picked up the puck and took off down the ice with it. He saw Johnson out of the corner of his eye, faked him out and dashed around him. He smiled to himself. At twenty feet out he let the puck go. It flew, MacPherson went down, the puck flew up and over his shoulder and into the net, much like a curve pitch in baseball.

The buzzer marked the end of the tie game. The crowd wouldn't settle down.

The boys sat on the bench or on the boards as the zamboni smoothed the ice. Rolle smiled at his team. "You guys seem to like overtimes," he grinned.

Jackie looked at him grimly, "This game is ours." His wrist was working overtime, sending pain impulses to his brain. He looked at Cookie, whose eye was swollen shut and had been for the entire game. He knew Cookie was seeing double, too, a little fact that was kept from Rolle. He hadn't even thought about Cookie's pain, whose eye was black now, making him look like a giant panda.

Duane was getting his glove retaped again, but he nodded in agreement with Jackie.

Rolle, an actor on an icy stage and superb in his performance, pulled out all the stops. This is where he shone, this was where he was at his all-time best. "Get that score," he said, "put the pressure on them!" Then, louder, "Forecheck the hell out them!" He turned to Cookie, Jim and Art, "Play defensively," he pleaded. "Hold them."

The Edina players skated on for the overtime. A mighty roar swept the arena. Thief River skated on. The roar was answered. Larry Johnson glided around the ice confidently; MacPherson coolly skated to his net. Jackie skated around hot-shot style trying to intimidate Johnson, who wasn't buying in.

The whistle blew. The contest was on. The puck was bouncing everywhere in front of Rod's net. Rod was white as a sheet and yelling at Fred and Duane to get on it. The puck settled for a split second and Ryan was on it like a fish snaps a fly. He flipped the puck into the net just as Duane pushed Johnson into the crease and pinned him up against the crossbar.

In the announcer's box Teigmeier sat stark quiet, then sadly spoke the sad words, "Goal, Edina wins."

Glen smashed his stick into the ice, crunching it. Splinters stuck out from the sides. He raced across the ice, hot tears streaming down his face, pushed the door open, jumped off the ice and ran down the stairs to the solace of the locker room.

The bulk of the crowd, like one terrifying monster, had collectively risen to its feet screaming either for or against the goal. The Prowler parents stood stun-gunned, superimposed on the mayhem. Paul Bedard leaned over to Tony Dorn, who stood next to him, and said thoughtfully, "An Edina player was in the crease. The goal should be disallowed." Tony nodded.

The Edina players emptied their bench and skated together in a green victory celebration.

At the same time a frantic short-legged referee was blowing his thin whistle over the din signaling no goal. The crowd noticed it first. It quieted. Then the players and coaches saw him. They quieted.

The referee picked up the puck and skated to the center of the ice for a face off.

The green crowd booed.

Suddenly the Thief River fans, including some who had left their seats and were standing in the aisles, connected with what was happening and started screaming in frenzied joy.

Larry Johnson skated to his coach in a rage. "He was pinning me against the crossbar!" he screamed.

McVeety chimed in, "How could he make a call like that?"

The see-saw had changed. The Prowlers faced a renewed chance. The crowd screamed. The unruly fans jumped up and down excitedly.

The referee motioned from center ice. The ice cleared and the players headed back on ice.

"Where's Glen?" Rolle bellowed.

There was a sobering moment when everyone looked for Glen like a lost mitten.

Chip was yelling over the crowd that was stuck on roar, trying to project his voice to reach Rolle's ears, "He thought we lost the game!" he screamed. "He skated off the ice!" Chip continued, yelling as loudly as he could, "I think he went to the locker room!"

For a fleeting moment Rolle looked crazy. "For Chrissake!" he yelled.

"I'll get him!" J.C. called over his shoulder as he was already running across the ice.

* * *

Overtime one...scoreless. Overtime two...scoreless.

As the boys headed on the ice for overtime three, thinking about last year's eleven overtime fiasco, Jackie said to Glen and Chip, "I'm tired of overtimes. Let's *score* for Christ's sake."

The period looked like the last two: brisk, cocky, well-played, and scoreless. Cookie still saw double. Jackie's wrist pain was unbearable. Duane lagged but he kept in there. Fred took up the slack and the two of them and Rod thwarted Johnson shot after shot after shot. The Edina defense and MacPherson did the same.

The crowd had screamed themselves hoarse. The parents sat pinned to the stiff seats in agony.

Then, Jackie got the puck. He didn't feel tired. The pain in his wrist evaporated. He felt only exhilaration. He knew where Chip was without looking. He could feel him moving swiftly off to his side, right where he was supposed to be. He acted like he didn't know where Chip was. He acted as if he, Jackie, was going down to make the shot. He chuckled inside himself as he kept a grim face for the Edina players. Without looking at Chip, or even making a motion toward him, Jackie flicked the puck to him.

Chip was ready. He knew exactly what Jackie would do. Chip picked up the pass, aimed and shot. The puck flew, screened by just about everyone green on the ice who tried to get between Chip and the goal. The puck was lost from sight. No one on either side, including MacPherson, saw it go into the net, but somehow it did.

34

"deliberate pause"

- William Shakespeare

Glen read the newspaper as he lay in bed after the game. His roommate, Jackie, had gone to the hospital with Rolle to have his wrist checked, but it was past curfew and J.C. had made sure everyone was in his room. Glen couldn't go to sleep until he knew how Jackie was.

When Jackie came back to the room, after midnight, his wrist was wrapped firmly in a professional bandage. Glen set his paper down neatly and looked tightly at Jackie, who tossed his jacket over a chair.

"You OK?" Glen questioned.

"It's sprained. It hurts like hell," he glowered. "Damn, that was a hit." Jackie started undressing with one hand, tossing his clothes randomly.

"How's Duane's hand?" Glen asked.

Jackie sighed as he clumsily pulled off his shirt, "The doctor restitched it again. He doesn't want Duane to play...says it can cause permanent damage." He undressed to his shorts and headed for the bathroom. Glen got up and followed. Jackie continued, "He doesn't know Duane!"

Jackie went in the bathroom and rummaged through his bag for his toothpaste and squeezed from the middle onto his toothbrush. Glen leaned against the door and looked at Jackie via his reflection in the glass over the sink. It was a big grand bathroom with huge puffy towels and little white and black tiles on the floor.

"Eveleth's going to be a rough game." Glen spoke but Jackie already knew this, of course. It was Glen's way of getting off a little nervous tension about tomorrow's game.

Jackie brushed heartily, "They've always played physical hockey," he said through the foam.

"Yeah, no one knows that better than we do!"

"I'm glad we're playing them," Jackie said resolutely as he spit out the foam, then continued as he rinsed his mouth, "They gave us the worst trouncing we ever had." He wiped his face with the plush towel and stuffed it in the towel rack. The toothpaste cover lay beside the toothpaste.

"I wish we were playing them with Cookie being able to see out of both eyes and not double out of one!" Glen said sadly as they walked back to the bedroom, "And with Jimmy...and with Duane's hand OK...and with your wrist in good shape." Glen sat on his twin bed neatly and pulled the covers over him. Jackie jumped in the other bed and looked defiant as he wrapped up in the blankets. "Bedard said we'd be ready if we worked hard," Jackie said, as he turned off the light, "...and we have!"

* * *

A banging on the door woke Glen up. Jackie, coming from a large family, could sleep through anything. Glen scrambled to the door and groggily unlocked it. In barged Art, Cookie, Chip, Duane, and Rod.

"You guys gonna sleep all day?" Chip smiled.

"Ugggghhh," Jackie answered from the rumpled bed.

Glen opened the curtains to a bright day as Duane wryly said, "How are you guys?"

Jackie yawned, acutely aware of the pain in his wrist, "It's you we're worried about."

More pounding on the door caused Jackie to put a pillow over his head. Art opened the door to Fred and Jim wearing funky beanies with a propeller on top. Everyone laughed. Then Cookie said, seriously, "You guys ready?"

Jackie threw the pillow at Cookie, "Yeah."

Rod interjected anxiously, his Pooh side showing. "We just saw the Eveleth guys, they look pretty confident."

Jim added, long faced, "I sure wish Jimmy was here. It's going to be a physical game..." He looked around the motley crew, "We sure could use his strength."

Jackie sat up in bed and grabbed his glasses from the end table with his unbandaged left hand. "We'll have to skate our asses off to make up for Jimmy being gone."

35

"the hounds of hell"

- William Shakespeare

The latecomers found their seats as the zamboni whirred off the ice. There was an acute charge etched into the air.

The door to the ice burst open as Gunderson skated out followed by Jerry Norman, Don "Twicky" Judnick, Jimmy Rossi, Gusty Hendrickson and James Drobnick. They were large, rough, tough, formidable boys who shot through the door like bullets. Their maroon and gold uniforms boasted "Eveleth Golden Bears." A roar of bawdy voices screamed for their team. The Eveleth band struck up their song. Jerry Norman was the star superior, eloquent as he rode his skates around the ice.

A matured Rod, but ever nervous before the game, skated out onto the ice. He smacked his gum unconsciously but his eyes were all business. The rest of the Prowlers followed suit looking as if they had a mission to fulfill. The crowd crescendoed behind them. Cookie's eye was swollen nearly shut, Duane's stick was taped to his glove, and Jackie was favoring his tightly wrapped wrist.

The Thief River Falls parents and townspeople were watching the boys from their seats in the screaming crowd. The band played the school pep song while the students sang.

Paul Bedard stood, edgy, proud of his proteges. He scrutinized each boy, then leaned over to Elmer Poole who stood next to him, "I'll bet those boys are thinking about the trouncing Eveleth gave them in the Pee Wee playoffs." Elmer shook his head as he scanned the Golden Bears, "Eveleth looks very strong."

Inside the glassy KTRF announcer's box, Teigmeier looked down at the rink like a watchful hawk eyeing its rabbit and said in deep tones that exuded excitement, "We're in for a barn burner tonight!" He sipped a cup of cocoa absently and rolled up his sleeves.

Eveleth was a mining town on the iron range located in the northeastern part of the state and was nothing like Thief River. Eveleth had a history of the high life when the mines were hot. Now the iron was raped, and the glory days were behind. But it had left behind a strong, tough generation and they loved hockey.

Rolle and J.C. sat together on the bench as Rolle talked to his team with deep feeling, "I know how badly you want this win. Now get out there and let Eveleth know!"

The referee dropped the puck between Jackie and Norman and the game was on. Jackie Poole and Jerry Norman, two superstars, both dug at it. Jackie won and passed it to Fred. Norman bent his knees low, followed Fred and caught up to him. Fred could feel Norman's hot breath on his neck as Norman mowed him down and stole the puck.

A few seconds later Drobnick smashed Glen into the boards. Glen saw the same nitty grin he remembered from Pee Wees spread across his face. It infuriated him.

Within a few seconds Chip was flattened by Rossi. And so it went, until Norman tripped Jackie. This one was so flagrant the referee didn't let it go. The whistle could be heard to the rafters. Norman skated off to the penalty box, surly and tough.

Glen, Jackie, Chipper, Duane and Fred skated together briefly before the face off as the referee retrieved a puck.

"Damn, they play rough hockey!" Glen said, winded.

Jackie narrowed his eyes furiously, "We've got to get one now with Norman off. He's brutal. That guy's everywhere."

"Let's go," Duane said in steely tones.

At the face off Jackie pushed the puck clumsily back to Duane. Duane gripped his stick and with total concentration whacked the puck toward the Eveleth net. The puck rocketed off his stick at the same moment the searing pain of his stitches, ripping open, traveled his body. Duane buckled to the ice in anguish as his well-aimed puck sailed past Gunderson and into the net.

Duane's father jumped out of his seat in pure ecstasy.

Teigmeier shouted about one half inch from the mike, "Duane Glass has scored from the blue line! The Thief River fans have gone crazy!"

The game was barely on again when Art received a penalty for an illegal check. Art was in the box and Chip was sitting on the bench when Jackie passed the puck to Glen. Drobnick was on Glen and a wild scramble for the puck ensued. Drobnick pulled back from Glen, gritting his teeth and setting his jaw, then elbowed Glen full force in the face. Everything inside Glen's head went silent. Blood spurted from his nose and the arena turned upside down as he fell and hit the ice. The blood formed a red and pinkish pool around his face. All he heard was a shrill whistle that stayed in his ears. Drobnick headed for the "sin bin"; Glen was helped off the ice.

Glen sat in the box with Rolle's face nearly pressed to his trying to determine the extent of damage to Glen's nose.

"I don't think it's broken," he heard Rolle say to J.C. Cookie was called for slashing. As the penalty was announced, the buzzer sounded throughout the St. Paul Auditorium. Period one was done and the score was 1-0 Prowlers.

* * *

In the locker room, the players were showing signs of wear. J.C. offered them Cokes and Hershey bars.

Duane peeked down his glove at his hand. He could feel the warm blood at the tips of his fingers, but it looked like it was matting now. The torn skin exposed his flesh and bone; it was odd, he couldn't remember what his hand felt like before the pain. It seemed as if it had been there forever. Rod looked at Duane and his hand, but didn't say anything.

Jackie held his wrist.

Cookie sat staring at the end of his skates. It looked like four skates instead of two. He was getting used to this.

Rolle changed the blood-soaked pads in Glen's nose and wiped Glen's face a bit to get some of the blood off.

"You alright?" he asked Glen.

"Yeah," Glen said, tasting blood down his throat.

Rolle looked at his squad. He didn't think they could keep up under the abuse, but the psychologist in him spoke to the boys. "Play defensively. We can't let them score. Keep Norman covered. He's dynamite...and above all...don't get any more injuries."

* * *

Back to play. The game was wild and the crowd was wild. The woolly Eveleth fans kept it going so loud no one could think. Fred got a penalty for holding Hendrickson, and it was hell to pay to keep the Bears from their score. Duane, Chip, Cookie and Glen played only defense.

"Shut him down, shut him down," Rod kept chattering, between gum smacks, to his teammates. And they did mostly, and the ones they didn't get, Rod got.

Judnick skated down ice chasing the puck. Glen, wads of soaked blood in his nose and blood smeared all over his face, got to it first and passed it to Chip. Judnick put on his brakes near the boards by the Eveleth net and swirled around to get back to the puck. Fred was racing toward the puck from the opposite direction as Judnick swirled, stick held high in the air. His stick smacked Fred full force on the forehead. Fred hit the ice dazed, blood oozing from his forehead as the sound from the whistle zanged through his ears. Fred got up, woozily, blood dripping from the wound.

"I'm OK," was all he said.

Judnick headed for the box.

Rolle and J.C. looked at Fred. "Oh no," Rolle lamented, "What's next?" Fred didn't come off the ice. He couldn't let the guys down. He felt dizzy.

In the bleachers, his parents brooded anxiously.

"He's weaving," his mother complained.

"He'll be OK. Fred has a level head on him," his father answered, but he was worried too.

The game wore on with no more scoring. Rolle anxiously prepped Jim, Cookie and Art before they went on the ice, "Everyone play defensively! Don't let them score!" All heads bobbed solemnly. Glen, Chip and Jackie came racing in for a line change. Jim, Cookie and Art went out.

Chip wiped his forehead with a sleeve as he piled over the boards. "This is the roughest game we've ever played," he said to J.C. "Those guys are crazy."

Jerry Norman skated down ice with the puck, Fred and Duane braced to stop him. Norman flicked the puck to Hendrickson, who passed it back.

Jim raced down the ice, his thoughts concentrating on Rolle's words. "Everyone play defensively. Don't let them score," rang in his ears. "Duane and Fred are both hurt," he thought, "and Cookie is seeing double...It's up to me..."

All Jim's energies were centered on not letting Norman score. Norman shot, giving it everything he had. Jim dove at the puck as it sailed toward Rod. Rod stopped the shot as Jim rode down the ice on his stomach, full speed, smashing into the solidly anchored goal pipe with his head. He was knocked unconscious, and as his body flipped around like a dead cat, his ribs smashed the goal post.

Teigmeier shouted from his perch, "Jim Hall has hit the post with his head! He's out cold! The Prowlers can't afford to lose a man."

Mr. and Mrs. Hall sat in the crowd, frantic. The blood drained from Mrs. Hall's face. Mr. Hall tightened his whole body and sat rigidly.

Mrs. Hall looked over to him, "We'd better go down."

Mr. Hall sat unmoving, "No."

Mrs. Hall became past frantic, "It's bad. He needs us."

Mr. Hall firmly replied, "We can't go."

Jim's girlfriend Janice sat with her hands covering her face, not looking. Her friend, Kay, reported to her what was happening on the ice.

The trainer and Rolle were getting Jim up and off the ice, onto the bench. He hung limply and barely conscious. Cookie and Art came off the ice.

The referee was anxious to get the game going. Jackie, Chip and Glen skated on.

Jackie barked to them, "We've got to strike now. They won't expect it." He looked at Glen, "I'll get it to you, shoot it back to Chip." He looked at Chip. "I'll get down ice for a pass or rebound."

They pulled it off like clockwork. Chip sent the perfect airborne pass to Jackie, who dropped it with his hand and calmly fired it into the net.

On the bench Rolle, J.C. and the trainer were bent over Jim, their backs to the ice action. The crowd was thundering.

Art screamed, "Jackie scored!"

Teigmeier, bristling with intensity, announced, "The Prowlers lead 2-0!"

Amid the yelling, Paul Bedard took a deep breath, puffed out his cheeks and let it out. He turned to his wife, Caroline. "They're going to do it. I just know it."

On the ice, bloody-faced Glen murmured to himself as he caught the puck on his stick, "One more. Let's go!" He skated the puck down the ice with long strides. The crowd was wild. Glen outskated the entire Eveleth team, feinted Gunderson to one side and shot on an open net, missing it. The crowd groaned.

Teigmeier gulped on his cocoa, raised his eyebrows and his voice went up an octave, "He missed! Carlson missed an open net!"

A few minutes later Clifford Thompson tripped Chip. The little referee blew his shrill, determined whistle. With Thompson in the box, Jackie and Chip ripped down the ice, faking everyone. Chip shot and Gunderson made a sensational save. The crowd gasped.

Art and Rossi collided and fell in front of the Eveleth net. Their skates tangled and they both struggled to get free from each other. A shrill whistle sounded as a cherry-faced referee skated angrily toward them.

Art said to Rossi, "Is he pointing at us?"

Rossi answered, "Sure as hell looks like it."

A voice on the loudspeaker echoed, "Penalties on Thief River No.

11, Art Cloutier, and Eveleth's No. 12, James Rossi. Two minutes each. Roughing."

Rossi and Art looked at each other and laughed. They giggled all the way to the penalty box together.

"That guy's crazy," Art said.

"He's an idiot," Rossi answered.

Rod was playing with a chunk of snow on the south end of the ice. He was bored and alone, with the action on the other end. He followed the chunk behind the net absently. Norman got a breakaway and headed for Rod, with Jackie chasing him. Rod didn't notice. Jackie looked toward the empty net. Rod peeked over it from behind. Fred and Duane were dashing to their positions. Norman shot just as Rod scrambled around in front of the net, stretched and caught Norman's puck baseball-style.

Rolle uttered a loud "Whew!" The crowd laughed, then cheered.

Rolle, J.C., Cookie, Jim, and Art were on the bench. Rolle towel-rubbed Jim's hair and talked to him softly.

"Can you take your shift, son?" Rolle asked. "Glen, Jackie and Chip need a few minutes rest."

"Yes," Jim bravely nodded, slurring his words thickly. "It only hurts when I breathe."

Rolle and J.C. looked at each other incredulously.

"Never mind," Rolle soothed, "we'll just keep shifting Art and Cookie in."

To J.C. he said, "Make the arrangements to get him to the hospital."

On ice, Glen saw his opportunity to set up a quick play to Chip, who barrowed the puck down the ice past everyone and scored on Gunderson point blank.

Rolle turned in time to see the goal and he thought about Thompson, Eveleth's coach. Eveleth was playing much better than the scoreboard showed, which was sometimes the case in hockey. He knew everything Thompson was thinking, everything he was saying. Rolle loved this soft spoken coach. As fate would have it, it hadn't been too many years before that Rolle played hockey for Eveleth under Thompson's tutelage. Now they were teacher and student, locking horns.

Rolle's game had been to wear Norman, the superstar, down.

* * *

The dim locker room had a guarded feeling between the second and third periods. J.C. had gone with Jim Hall and his parents to the emergency room of the hospital and so far there was no word on his condition.

Rolle warned the players not to let up for a moment. "Jerry Norman could get a hat trick in no time. We don't have this game won yet. Play defensively. All we've got to do is keep them tied up so they can't score."

Rolle looked at the players, but there was nothing more he could say. At this point they had one common goal and nothing he could say would make them want it more. They were reduced to one line now with two players shifting in. He knew they were as tired as Napoleon's retreating soldiers and had to conserve their energy as much as possible. It would be a total defensive grind to keep the Golden Bears from scoring in the third period.

And that is what they did.

36

"you've gotta have heart"

Spread out on a rumpled scarlet bedspread, in the room of the St. Paul Hotel, was a newspaper full of Prowler pictures and a lengthy article about their win over Eveleth. Jackie, Glen and Duane huddled around it. Jackie's wrist was bandaged, Duane's hand wrapped in new bandages. Glen's black and blue eyes were underlined with a very white bandage over his nose.

Jackie said excitedly, "What does it say?"

Glen read for a moment, then looked up at his chums. "It says we're rugged!"

Jackie and Glen smiled at each other.

Duane read out loud, "Defenseman Duane Glass who teamed with Fred Dablow at the blue line to keep the Eveleth Golden Bears from taking any good shots..."

"Hey, look at this!" Jackie beamed. "They're calling us 'the team with heart'!"

Rod, Chip, Art, Jim, Fred, and Cookie came in the unlocked door without knocking. Fred's bandage covered his forehead and Cookie's eye was still swollen shut, but now yellow and purple instead of black.

"Jim! How you doing?" Jackie asked.

Jim answered sheepishly, in obvious pain, "I've got three broken ribs." He drew a slow and painful breath. "It hurts to breathe but they're taped. I can play."

Jackie shook his head, then turned to Chip. "Ready to skate out under those lights tonight, Chipper?"

"You better believe it!" Chip answered. "All these years and now that it's almost here it doesn't seem possible."

Rod asked Duane, "How's your hand?"

Duane winced, "It's sewed up again. The doc says if the stitches come out again there's no skin left to stitch!"

"Geez," Glen commented, but couldn't think of anything more to say.

"How's the eye, Cook?" Jackie asked.

Cookie answered, "Fine," but everyone knew better.

Jim gravitated to the newspaper. "You guys got a paper! We tried to get one. They're sold out!"

"Let's go down to the lobby," Rod suggested. "Everyone's there and we'll be celebrities!" He eyed Glen. "Angie's down there, Glen."

Glen blushed. Jackie jumped on this one. He stood up, his hand over his chest and lilted in his girl voice, "Oh, Glen." He batted his lashes, "You're so cute in your hockey uniform...all those muscles!"

All the boys laughed, including Glen, as they piled out of the room.

The opulent lobby was jammed full of fans, parents, families, the press, and players from all the teams. It looked like the wrong set got put up behind the wrong scene.

As they got off the elevator, an excited knot of people was gathered around Oscar Mahle, the superstar from International Falls, the team the Prowlers would play for the championship. Oscar Mahle looked cool, collected and every bit the star.

Glen wasn't interested in Mahle. He scrutinized the crowd, anxiously looking for Angie. He saw her chatting with a group of girls and broke off from his teammates, winding through the tangled masses toward her.

No one thronged him or any of the Thief River players. They weren't recognized.

"Hi, Angie," Glen said behind her. She started, then turned and brightened.

"Well, hi," she answered.

"Let's find somewhere quiet," he said, pulling her through the crowd. They found a corridor and pushed through a door which landed them in a deserted, dark and strangely quiet ballroom.

"I've missed you," Glen said.

Angie looked at his taped nose. "You OK?" she asked.

"Yeah."

"I thought your nose was broken."

"So did I."

"How is it?" She put her hand lightly on the bandages and Glen leaned toward her.

"Does he kiss as well as he plays hockey?" Chip's voice echoed through the ballroom.

Glen and Angie jerked back as Chip appeared out of the shadows with Rosalie Fonnest, a lovely, full-lipped, brown haired beauty that he had had a crush on for years. They both looked radiantly happy.

Glen stayed close to Angie.

Angie smiled at the intruders, "Ready for the game tonight, Chip?"

Chip answered with merriment in his eyes, "I guess I'd better be. We've been working our whole lives for it!"

37

"this above all,
to thine own self be true"

- William Shakespeare

The Prowler hockey team entered the dingy locker room at the St. Paul Auditorium for the final game of the 1956 season. They came quietly, hungrily. It was different from the other games because of the feeling of finality riding the air. No one said it, but it was there.

J.C. carried in Jim's gear. Duane's dad brought in Duane's. The hockey jackets were hung in the lockers and the ritual of dressing for the game began.

As the hockey bags opened it was clear that it was good the season was over. The stench was as bad as a Portuguese fish market; the boys hadn't washed their hockey clothes since the St. Paul Johnson game.

Jim gritted his teeth and grimaced in pain as Fred helped him get his shirt off, revealing an entire chest wrapped in bandages. Jackie and Duane functioned clumsily. Duane's father, Rolle and J.C. spent time going from boy to boy helping where they could.

Cookie's now-yellow eye had opened some and the pupil glared out from the slit. Glen's blackened eyes contrasted with the stiff white bandage over his nose. Fred's gash was exposed across his forehead because he didn't like the feel of the bandage. Grim ancient mariners couldn't have looked more terrible.

Rolle slid out of the stuffy locker room and leaned against the corridor wall, lost in thought. J.C. saw him and followed suit. It was deserted in the hallway but the boisterous opponents, the International Falls team, could be heard behind a door down the hall. But here the two men were alone.

"You OK, Dennis?" J.C. queried.

Rolle's thought wheels were turning like a lathe as he answered, "I've never wanted to win so much in my life." He focused on J.C., the stalwart who had been there for him both seasons, without pay, without official thanks. He froze with them at Baudette, cried with him over Jimmy, felt their pain, and shared in their joy.

"I know," J.C. answered steadily.

"Look at those kids," Rolle said gruffly. "We're going out for the state championship game, and it looks like a hospital ward in there." They looked at each other, two fine men who had gotten swept along with the crazy goal of a group of obstinate kids, faithful generals of depleted rebel troops before the battle.

"At least we have our own jerseys, they don't have to dress under the bleachers in a gym or in a coal room, and we can play indoors," J.C. tried to lighten the moment.

They looked at each other with a deep bond. "We've been through so much, J.C.," Rolle reminisced. "Can you believe it was a year ago we played that ill-fated eleven overtime game in the Harding jerseys?"

"This *week* seems like a year!" J.C. answered.

As the men slipped back into the locker room, the boys were dressed and sitting quietly on the benches with their own thoughts. Fred had just finished tying Jim's skates, Duane's father was putting the finishing touches on taping his son's stick to his glove, Glen had laced Jackie's skates and was sitting himself down on a bench.

Rolle stood looking solemnly at his scant, anxious-to-get-on-with-it team. His thoughts went back to the first day of practice on the pond when his hopes were just to win half their games. He wanted to tell them to be satisfied if they lost, to be happy that they made it this far, but from the look of determination that defied reason he saw in their eyes, he knew that was not the thing to say, not now. He could not imply to them to be less than they, in their stubborn minds, thought that they were. He must say what they needed to hear and say it with relish.

He skimmed the boys for a moment and his eyes rested on Jackie. How different he was from a year ago. He hadn't aspired to be the team leader and didn't have the qualities one would pick for a leader, and yet not only was he the leader, he was awesome at it. Jackie inspired his teammates on the ice.

He looked smaller and vulnerable right now as he gathered his strength.

Glen demanded perfection of himself and got it. He knew his shot, knew his opposition, knew his strengths and used them.

Glen, the all-American athlete, was sure of himself, calculating and ready.

Chip looked like a fenced colt itching for the freedom of pasture beyond. He would skate wild and free on the ice, finding the holes and darting through them. He would be where Jackie knew he would be. Chip would give his all for his team, his friends and his town.

The god, Mercury, couldn't perform better than Chip.

Duane was still the lone wolf off ice, but, on this team, he had drawn into the pack. He was tough, not strong in the same way as Cookie, but tough with a deep resiliency and no one messed with Duane. He had proven to be a top notch teacher with Fred under his wing, making Fred a first-rate defenseman. He had withstood pain stoically and would do anything for the team.

Duane looked agitated.

Fred had risen to the occasion presented to him by the fates. He was tall and inherently slow moving but had learned Duane's tricks to perfection, rarely making a mistake. He was able to endure the long stretches on the ice with Duane.

Fred looked wise, tired and apprehensive.

Jim had had a rough week losing Jimmy and dealing with his broken ribs and concussion from hitting the post. He had been in the limelight one year on Joey's line, then had to start over this year and build a rapport with Cookie and Jimmy. They had created a great line before the bottom dropped out. He never complained and never let his teammates down.

Jim had become the Roman warrior who had just won the last battle and was ready for the next. He had mastered self discipline and inner strength, and proved unflinching under pressure.

Rod looked like a small boy you wanted to hug. He had grown and matured, but everyone intuitively took Rod under wing. Rod depended so much on Duane and his other teammates that somehow he never realized his own greatness. He shared loyalty and worked hard with every one of them.

Rod was chewing his gum so fast Rolle thought his jaw would seize.

Cookie waited, involuntarily flexing his muscles like the Spanish bull before the fight. My God, what this untamed spirit had become, Rolle mused. Cookie's complacency and disgust for him, Rolle, had metamorphosed into total commitment toward the team.

Cookie was a force to be reckoned with.

Art had taken up a banner too big for him, but he was refusing to buckle under its weight. He shared their dream and would put every ounce of his being into helping realize it.

Art was introspective and ready for the big challenge.

There was no fleeting moon here, Rolle thought. Each boy would work to his capacity and far beyond. No matter what the outcome, he knew they would be able to hold their heads up. Rolle's concern, as he started his speech, was just how long they could physically hold up against the dynamite International Falls team.

J.C. moved back against the wall and Rolle moved to his usual space between the two benches, acutely aware that this would be his last speech to this group that had a grip on his heart. He looked at the waiting boys and they looked back at him expectantly.

Rolle took a big breath and sighed. "They're calling you 'the team with heart'," he began, then continued, choking up, "I call you the best damn team to ever hit the state of Minnesota." He lowered his voice for control. "We're in for the roughest game we've ever played against the toughest team we've ever faced..." he paused and looked full at these phenomenal boys with no common sense, "...and I believe that we can beat them."

38

under the lights

Except for softly lit exit signs it was pitch black, but the roar of the crowd was stupendous.

In the box, Rod waited, revving up on Doublemint.

The P.A. system crackled momentarily, then a strong male voice announced, "For Thief River Falls, No. 1, Rod Collins in the nets." Doots rolled the drums. Spotlights flashed on Rod, who skated out under them toward center ice as the Thief River band played. A deafening roar followed him as he skated to center ice snapping his gum.

The system crackled again and then the voice announced, "For Thief River Falls, No. 4, Jim Hall, center." The drums rolled again. Jim skated out stiffly, unconsciously holding his ribs with his arm as the cheers and band music followed him.

"For Thief River Falls, No. 6, Jack Poole, center," the voice boomed and Jackie was out the door, to his drum roll, hot rodding toward Rod and Jim as the lights danced around him. The roof 'blew off' the arena.

Chip, standing behind Glen, leaned over to his friend. They could see each other by the spotlight that was carrying Jackie to center ice. Tears streamed down Chip's face. "We're going to do it, Glen! We're finally going to do it!"

The light snapped off. The announcer continued, "For Thief River Falls, No. 7, Glen Carlson, left wing." The drums rolled and Glen skated out with his long, low strides. He was pumped up to the max, but a feeling of gratitude that they actually made it overlaid the excitement. He followed the beacon and heard the muffled band through the roaring crowd that was screaming him out to center ice.

"For Thief River Falls, No. 8, Clifford Strand, right wing," the voice announced. There was a moment of absolute silence as no one recognized the name, then a giant boom of approval as the drummer drummed, and Chip flashed out under the lights, grinning ear to ear. The crowd was not aware of his tears.

"For Thief River Falls, No. 9, Duane Glass, defense," the voice announced in the same tone. The drums rolled. Duane skated on, tough and sure of himself. The crowd exploded as the light carried him out and the band played on. Duane was hugged by his teammates at center ice.

The crowd had all been on their feet clapping, whistling and cheering through the pomp. Mr. Glass and Paul Bedard clasped hands and looked at each other with a shared pride over the boys.

"For Thief River Falls, No. 11, Art Cloutier, left wing," the voice continued. Art stepped onto the ice like it was eggs. He heard the drum roll and smiled through the cheers as he glided through the light. He had risen to the occasion the fates had dished him and he skated with pride as he heard his cheers and his band playing for him.

"For Thief River Falls, No. 12, Fred Dablow, defense," the voice droned. Doots rolled her drums as Fred stepped out under the spotlights and glided flawlessly to his team as the heady crowd screamed madly over the band.

"And, for Thief River Falls, No. 14, Ronald Reese, right wing!" The drummer rolled her final tribute as Cookie heaved his huge body out the door and to the center of the ice, the lights playing around him. The zealous band played and the crowd cheered to its capacity.

"And their coach, Dennis Rolle!" The lights shot on Rolle and J.C. in the box. They stood humbly as Rolle smiled and waved up to the crowd.

The lights flashed once more to center ice. All the boys hugged and in the stands all the cheerers cheered, and when the announcer said, "Let's play hockey!" the screaming couldn't get any louder.

39

international falls

periods 1 and 2

The teams huddled briefly as the fans got set for the thriller they knew they were about to witness: the battered Thief River Falls team that seemed unstoppable and the powerhouse, International Falls.

In the International Falls huddle, Oscar Mahle reassured his teammates, "We'll keep our heads together and do what we've done all year." The others nodded and he, Bob Laurion, Larry Cronkhite, Elmer Walls, David Frank and Thomas Neveaux, with his black eye swollen shut, skated out onto the ice to the roar of their fans.

On the other side of the ice Rolle instructed Duane and Fred, "You've got to shut down Oscar Mahle. He can skate and shoot. Watch that backhand of his, it's brutal."

He turned to Jackie and Chip, "Walls doesn't make mistakes. Use your speed to get around him."

In the announcer's box Doug Teigmeier was warming up, "...championship game between the Thief River Falls Prowlers and the International Falls Broncos. The atmosphere is absolutely charged. The sensational Oscar Mahle will be on ice against our own phenomenal Jack Poole..."

To a great roar the referee dropped the puck. Jackie had never felt so focused in his life. Nothing mattered except winning this game. The pain in his wrist was annoying, but he would conquer it.

His split-second reflexes won the face off, like his childhood idol Bud Brussoit, and just as fast as Bud, he fired it back to Duane. He knew Duane was ready. Duane was always ready. Jackie saw Duane awkwardly shove the puck to Glen who started down ice with it, surely, neatly, methodically.

Glen saw Chip break, lightning fast, toward the net. Glen aimed a long sure pass to Chip, who agilely sidestepped Walls and in one fluid movement caught, then drilled, the puck past Laurion and into the left corner of the net. Eight seconds had elapsed on the clock. The goal took less than eight seconds, but it took the flustered clock keeper a couple seconds to actually stop the clock.

The boys fell into each other's arms and then into a heap on the ice to the ear splitting, background blaring of the crowd. Doots efficiently rolled her drums and the Thief River band played the familiar school song; the voice on the loudspeaker announced Chip's score;   the screamers screamed; the yellers yelled; the whistlers whistled; the student body sang the song. In short, the stunned crowd went crazy.

Rod, alone on his end of the ice, looked up at the booming, screaming, psychedelic wave upon wave of arms and bodies. He skated in towards his teammates for the celebration, waving his stick and yelling but not being heard over the commotion.

On the bench Jim, Art, Cookie, J.C., and Rolle were ecstatic. In the background the cheerleaders led the fans in "Two bits, four bits, six bits a dollar! All for Thief River stand up and holler!" The lid was off.

Jackie's parents hugged. The younger brothers and sisters bobbed up and down.

Paul Bedard said to Mr. Glass, "Bet that sets a record, eh?"

Mrs. Strand and Mrs. Collins sat amid the crowd primly. Mrs. Strand smiled, "That Chipper's pretty good, huh?"

"He surely is, Palma," Mrs. Collins agreed.

* * *

And home in Thief River, in the parish house, Father Noah's eyebrows flew up as he listened to Teigmeier's broadcast.

* * *

The game turned into a free-for-all. Both teams wanted a goal desperately, Thief River to protect their score and International Falls to tie the game. Oscar Mahle was the fastest skater they'd encountered from any other team. Like Chip, the opposing team never knew where he was going to turn up.

Mahle had the puck and skated greased-fast down the ice with it. He stopped and started to fire a backhand shot toward the net. Duane was slightly in front of Mahle and to his side. The only thought in Duane's mind was his job...*stopping that puck*. He knew how fast and how accurate it would be if Mahle got it off.

Duane lunged in a dive to stop the puck. At the same moment Mahle hit the puck *and* Duane, whacking him full in the face. Duane's body jerked up a second and then fell, blood spurting from his nose.

In the crowd his father gasped, "Oh, no," and his mother bit her lip. The Thief River side was quiet as butter. On the ice Duane got up growling, with his 'mad bear' look billboarded, so even the watchers in the peanut gallery got the picture.

"I'm OK," he mouthed to his concerned teammates as he skated to the bench, blood pouring from his nose.

The crowd applauded, yelled, and screamed its support for their hero Duane.

Duane came back in to play, with wads of cotton stuffed up his nose. His hand had novocaine shots right before the game that deadened the pain for awhile. His main problem, for the moment, was not his hand or his face. It was that his stick was so hard to handle with his glove so firmly taped to it.

* * *

The pace of play didn't let up.

Mahle wanted a goal. He tried all his tricks but Duane, Fred and Rod were a step ahead of him.

Billy Cronkhite had the puck and breezed toward Fred and Duane. Billy zipped the puck to Mahle who skated in, setting himself up for a goal.

Duane rushed in and tripped him, chuckling.

The referee didn't see the humor. His whistle resounded throughout the arena and Duane was sent to the penalty box for two minutes.

Rolle gathered his team briefly and said tersely, "Cookie, go in for Chip. Take Duane's position. Your size'll scare them if you're on defense. *Everyone* play defense. Tie up Mahle. They'll be trying everything they can to get a goal with Duane off the ice."

The minutes near the end of the first period were played tenaciously. Cookie and Fred crunched everyone they could into the boards, while Jackie and Glen belted the pucks into Laurion. Mahle pelted Rod with a series of little shots that Rod swatted away like an old pro.

Mahle was mad and frustrated, but kept his cool and did not draw a penalty.

Duane's penalty ended. The Prowlers held their lead and the buzzer signaled the end of the first period. Teigmeier reported to his radio audience, "That wraps up the end of the first period of play here at the State Championship game. This period was certainly right up there with the finest play the State Championship has ever seen. For those of you just tuning in, the score is 1-0 Prowlers at the end of the first period."

* * *

The crowd kept up its level of excitement but had quieted between periods to eat and drink and be ready. In the locker room the feeling was "up" but no one was about to let his guard down.

"Remember," Rolle told them, "in hockey things can happen fast and one goal ahead isn't safe, especially with Oscar Mahle and his troops on the ice."

They already knew this, but Rolle saying it made it more urgent.

"How are those ribs, Jim?" Rolle asked.

Jim nodded, indicating he would make it.

Rolle knew the suffering Jim was enduring. Every breath, every movement, sent racking pain shuddering through his body.

To Chip, Glen and Jackie he said, "We've got to outmaneuver them and get another one."

Duane's brows were knit into his forehead as he looked down at his glove. The hand pain had become part of him, like a leaf turning from green to yellow. It was just there, always throbbing, unless the pain killers had been injected.

The numbness was almost as bad because then his hand was not painful, it was dead, useless.

"Rod," Rolle's wide smile glittered at his goalie, "You're doing great." Rod grinned contentedly like Pooh after he had emptied the honey jar.

Duane pulled his hand out of his glove when Rolle turned his head to see how much time was left before the period started. The bandage was soaked with blood.

Jackie looked at Duane's hand soberly. "This wasn't how we planned to play the championship game, was it?"

* * *

The buzzer sounded to start the second period. Back and forth and back and forth the teams went down the ice. Neither team scored but magnificent playing electrified the crowd.

Then Glen got the puck and smoothly and swiftly stick handled it down the ice. Walls slid into position in front of Glen, but Glen foresaw his move and slapped the puck sideways to Jackie. Jackie razzle dazzle skated and stick handled, dodged Neveaux and shot a snappy backhand into the net. As the puck settled behind Laurion the Thief River crowd, hoarse from days of yelling, crescendoed again in deafening, ear splitting joy. Doot's drum roll and the band, who was faithfully playing the Prowler pep song, couldn't be heard more than ten seats away.

2-0 Prowlers!

The little group of parents jumped up and down and Mrs. Poole chanted, "I can't believe it! I can't believe it!" Mrs. Carlson smiled at her and Mr. Carlson shook Mr. Poole's hand.

Oscar Mahle had had enough. He found himself thirty feet out from Rod and was off balance, but that pesky Duane wasn't quite on him so he shot the puck in toward the net. In the Prowler effort to stop the puck it was screened. Rod saw it just as it buzzed by his nose. Mahle scored and it was a jubilant International Falls' turn to celebrate.

Now that Mahle knew he could get the puck past the Prowler defense and Rod, he was raring to get another one. The game was half over. There was plenty of time. Like a shark he circled Rod's net, waiting for his opportunity.

Oscar Mahle was eighteen feet out in front of the net and his stick was pulled back to make a backhand shot.

Duane, on him, maneuvered to 'sweep check' Mahle but could not gain control of his numb hand. As Duane swept he lost his balance and went sprawling face first on the ice. The puck whizzed by him and by Rod, smack into the Prowler goal.

Pandemonium was on the agenda again with the International Falls group. Their purple and gold flew everywhere. Teigmeier was screaming, "Tie game! Tie game!" to his northern radio audience.

Fred skated over to Duane, who was angrily getting up. "I'm tired of this ga-damn bandage. I can't control shit!"

Duane raced to the bench and shouted to Rolle as he climbed over the boards, "I need a rest." He didn't look at Rolle. Rolle looked oddly at J.C. but didn't say anything to Duane. Duane had never before asked for a rest.

Rolle called out, "Cookie, go in for Duane."

Duane took off his glove and started unwrapping the bandages that held his hand together.

Art, sitting next to him, said, aghast, "What are you doing?"

The others were watching the game and not paying attention to Duane. Duane didn't answer but continued unwrapping. The hand was yellow, purple and black. The secured stitches were black. Bumps of dried and fresh blood stained the hand where it had seeped through the stitches. Jim looked over and saw what was going on.

"Jesus, Duane," he protested.

High in the bleachers, behind the Prowlers' bench, Duane's anxious parents watched the scenario. "Oh, lord," his mother intoned.

Duane jammed his hand back into his glove, got up stoically, slid by Art, Jim and J.C., up to Rolle. "I'm ready," he announced.

Rolle was not aware of what Duane had done. He yelled, "Cookie!" and motioned him off the ice. Cookie came off like a boxcar with no brakes and Duane said to him gruffly, "Thanks, Cook."

Cookie nodded brusquely, Cookie style.

Duane skated on the ice to Fred. "They're not scoring any more goals," he said solemnly.

The score remained 2-2 at the end of the second period.

40

"when the battle's lost and won"

- William Shakespeare

Both teams retired to the tight, dim locker rooms. The Thief River locker room was eerily quiet. A lifetime rode on one period. J.C., unaware of the unbandaged hand inside Duane's glove, was taping the stick anew to his glove with the throbbing hand snugly inside it.

Fred sat hunched over and suddenly felt exhausted. He had skated nearly every shift of every game all year. These last five games had been brutal. Jim was wrung out. Glen was tired, Chip's tired eyes were bloodshot, and so it went.

Rolle felt the slump. It was up to him to get them glued back together. "They're getting hot," Rolle said steadily. "You've got to get a goal and you've got to hold them." His voice grew more intense, "Mahle will be coming out like gangbusters. They won't give anything. It will have to be stolen."

* * *

The two teams skated onto the ice for the third period to a standing ovation. The cold exhilarated the teams, giving them a second wind. Jackie and Frank faced off. The puck ended up with Chip, who ripped down ice toward Laurion. Mahle cut him off just as Chip was going to shoot. Mahle spent time in the box. He made the move he had to, sacrificing himself to save a sure goal.

"We've got to score now while they're shorthanded," Glen said to Chip.

But they didn't. International Falls held them for the two minutes and when Mahle came back out, he was ready to score again.

Art got the puck. A shiver went through his body as he eyed the net. He had a chance to score but Bob Miggins zoomed in and high sticked him. It was Miggins' turn for the box.

"We've got to score now while they're shorthanded," Jackie prodded Glen and Chip.

But they didn't. The Broncos stopped everything the Prowlers gave them.

Cookie didn't seem to be in focus, Rolle thought desperately. He hadn't really been the same since the Roseau game when the puck hit him under the eye. Duane's hand would be throbbing intensely as the novocaine wore off. He saw Jim sorely puffing down the ice with his broken ribs. The concussion he sustained when his head hit the pipe must be giving Jim problems also. He knew Jackie's wrist was sore.

Rolle saw it slipping away. It was asking too much for Fred and Duane to be on the ice all the time. These last games were just too much.

Rolle shook off his thoughts as he watched Jackie skating like the wind down the glaring ice sheet.

Mahle joined him center ice and tripped him. Mahle was off to the penalty box again.

"We've got to do it now!" Rolle pleaded.

Perhaps, perhaps, but Wall was a wall, Laurion was formidable and the two minutes ticked off with no goal. The rest of the International Falls team played like wild eagles protecting their nest when Mahle was off.

Mahle got out of the box and latched on.to the puck. He skated almost directly for Cookie. Cookie let him almost pass, then tripped him.

With Cookie in the box the Broncos saw their chance.

Rolle screamed, "Defense! Defense!" The Thief River crowd took up the chant.

Rod kept chewing his worn-out gum. He had performed to his zenith but he couldn't stop to think about that now. One mistake would cost the game. He couldn't take those nightmares for another year.

Now came Oscar Mahle again, bent on scoring.

Duane skated toward Mahle. Rolle stiffened as he watched. Duane planned his move and came in on Mahle, checking him mid ice, just inside the blue line. Mahle flipped over in the air, circus style, from the force of the check and lay momentarily knocked out.

In the announcer's box Teigmeier reported, "This is no game for the feint of heart..."

The minutes ticked away. It appeared that the game would end in a tie. The action focused around the International Falls net. Rod stood alone at the other end. For no apparent reason, Rod started skating to the Thief River bench. Rolle, J.C., Jackie, Chip and Glen were watching the action by the International Falls net at the other end of the ice. Rod skated up undetected by them.

Chip was yelling encouragement, "Get it in there, Jim!"

Glen glanced toward the clock, which was behind the Thief River net, and saw Rod skating up. "*What's wrong? What's wrong?*" Glen screamed.

Jackie, Chip, J.C., and Rolle all turned, horrified to see Rod standing there.

"Nothin', I'm thirsty..." Rolle turned ruby red and screamed, "Get back! Get back!"

Rod, looking like a beloved puppy who had just been chastised, turned dejectedly and skated back, just as the action turned. Mahle was intently starting down ice with the puck and he was all business.

Rod skated as fast as his legs would carry him. The Prowler crowd was screaming frantically. He got there just in time to save the shot.

Rolle was perspiring. The pressure had gotten to Rod, he had flipped out...who would be next?

Mahle got the puck from Frank at the face off. He skated toward the net grimly determined and totally engrossed in his task, which was to score.

Duane had time to position himself as Mahle flew up. Duane dropped onto his knees, gripped his stick with both hands and swept the puck from Mahle just as Mahle's stick hit Duane's stick, ripping off the attached glove.

The stick and glove went flying across the ice. Duane's face tightened up in agonizing pain. He grabbed his hand. The stitches were torn and blood poured out of the wound. The novocaine was completely gone so Duane got the benefit of full pain.

Jim retrieved Duane's stick and glove. He had to bend over splitting in pain to pick them up. He brought them to Duane, who was willing his tuckered body to get up. His body responded slowly.

Jim eyed Duane's hand, "Christ Almighty, Glabbo!"

"Give me those before Rolle sees," Duane snarled. Duane grabbed his glove and jammed the bleeding hand into it. Jim, Cookie, Fred and Art gathered around him.

No one said anything, but just looked at each other in the perfect understanding of a mission that must be completed.

On the bench Glen, Chip and Jackie sat anxiously, waiting for their shift. Chip and Glen hooted and hollered as their teammates played. Jackie, between them, was deep in thought.

He remembered himself hanging over the boards watching Bud and Bob with the other little boys and remembered saying, "I'm going to be like Brussoit someday...tricky."

His memory twined to Chip telling them, excitedly, about skating out under the lights and how he had said, "I just want to skate there and win."

He recalled Father Noah on the river, "Learn to discipline yourself, draw out the goalie..."

He thought back on the Thieves game when they were kids and Chip, who said, in an innocent child's voice, "Can we ever be like that?" "You bet your ass we can," he remembered answering. So cocky. So cocky.

He recollected Pee Wees and the lessons learned from Paul Bedard who had taught them fastidiously, then told them, "There's a lot to the game of hockey..." Boy, was he right, Jackie thought wryly.

He came back to the present as Glen and Chip were all but mauling him.

"Come on! We've gotta get out there!" they yelled. "Let's go! Let's go!"

Rolle shot a sideways glance at the ruckus. "Oh, God," he thought, seeing Jackie's fogged look, "now we've lost Jackie."

Jackie skated out to meet Frank for the face off. He should have seen the puck but instead he saw himself throwing his hockey stick at the clock, "I'm sick of this bullshit," he screamed.

He felt Frank's power as the puck dropped, but Jackie's quickness won it by rote. Chip had the puck safely on his blade, but skidded it back to Jackie as he broke toward the net. Jackie caught the puck and skated down ice, skating low. His father's face blazed before him. Jackie was saying to him, and he could still feel his pain, "Dad, will I ever be as good as Joey, as Joey, as Joey..."

Jackie passed the puck to Duane who shot it up to Glen, who passed it back to Jackie. What masters they all had become, he thought.

The International Falls players loomed large before him. He dodged one and smiled as he remembered, "Pum, pum pullaway!"

He passed the puck to Glen who zapped it and passed to Chip. They were the ice gods now.

He saw Jimmy's face behind the old arena, "...ain't nothin' more important than winnin' State."

Jackie was racing for the net and saw Chip with the puck behind the net. A huge grin spread across Chip's face as he passed the black disc to Jackie. As the puck skimmed across the ice the background noise was blocked out. Jackie heard only Rolle's tunneled voice in his head, "...and I believe that we can beat them."

Thud. The puck hit his stick. He felt it but didn't hear it. Jackie saw Laurion concentrating on the puck at the same time Jackie was drawing him out.

For a split second Jackie toyed with the puck. He felt a smile, inside him, that came from deep inner satisfaction. He took what seemed to him a slow and deliberate aim, almost slow motion.

* * *

In the crowd his father whispered in a hushed, hope-filled voice, "That's it, son, that's it..."

* * *

Joey was on his feet at the bowling rink under the student union at the University of North Dakota as he watched on a small black and white television set. "Come on, Jackie!" he screamed.

* * *

Then Jackie drilled the puck into the net behind Laurion, who knew he'd been had.

* * *

Father Noah sat in his chair still listening to his small brown radio and absently playing with the folds in his robes. Teigmeier was absolutely hysterical, "...draws out Laurion...and...yes, YES! Jackie Poole has scored!"

The priest leaped from his chair and jumped up and down.

* * *

As the puck hit the net and settled on the ice, the crowd exploded. Jackie turned, stick poised in the air, and faced his teammates triumphantly. Chip ran on the tips of his rockered skates toward Jackie, stick as high in the air as he could get it. Glen spun wildly and headed for Jackie. Duane stood numbly on the ice for a split second, then all his pain drained from his body as he skated furiously toward his friends. Fred let out a whoop as he skated in and Rod, throwing his stick high in the air, lumbered down ice to his teammates.

They met in a mighty collision and fell to the ice in one scrambled pile. Jim, Cookie and Art clamored over the boards, skated out and smashed into the pile. Rolle and J.C. ran out on the ice. The crowd combusted into screams.

Amid the turmoil, Jackie saw Miss Skomedahl's face in his mind, he saw the kind smile in her eyes, and he heard his own voice saying:

> *"When the hurly burly's done,*
> *When the battle's lost...and won!"*

As Miss Skomedahl's face faded out Jackie grasped the moment. All the players, including Cookie, had tears streaming down their faces. So did Rolle and J.C.

Jackie, squished at the bottom of the pile, managed a delirious, "We did it!" as he hugged Duane.

The crowd was crying, yelling, screaming in homage to a battered group of boys with heart, with grit, with hope, with never-give-up determination...the bare bones team that somehow believed in itself enough to overcome every adversity fate threw at it. The boys who wouldn't let anything or anyone stand in the way of their goal. The unlikely rag tags who were willing to work and sacrifice to achieve their dream, the 1956 Thief River Falls Prowlers, who were the champions.

Postlogue

The wind-swept river is alone now. The boys are gone and no replacements took up the vigil. But when I went there on a cold winter day nearly forty years later I could hear their voices etched in the wind like a conch shell...echoing, echoing the sounds of hockey.

a note of gratitude

thank you to everyone
who shared the material
that made it possible to write this book
and especially to Glen Carlson
who gave me the frame on which to hang the story
and who was always there with encouragement

thank you to my family
who lived a topsy-turvey life
through its writing

thank you to my husband
for financing this venture over many years

thank you to my friends
old and new
who had faith in this project

thank you "boys" for having the guts to live the story
that tales are made of

thank you, Colleen and David,
for editing it

thanks to Ed MaGaa
for the first printing

Afterword

The magic of the Prowlers lived into the writing of this book. I realized this with my first goosebumps from Duane Glass, the first person I contacted about my decision to document their story, who said, in a husky voice, "It was a very special experience...almost spiritual." This feeling permeated every Prowler I spoke with, then spread to everyone else I interviewed.

My family lived in Wilmette, Illinois, a suburb of Chicago, during the writing of the screenplay, which was the form *River of Champions* was first written. On our first trip my daughter, Colleen, son, Andy and I traveled to Thief River Falls in the dead of winter to the warmth of the people who greeted us and took us into their hearts. Paul Bedard took Colleen and Andy ice fishing on the Thief River, Art Cloutier drove us anywhere we wanted to go and his son, Alex, Andy's age, and Andy struck up a wonderful relationship. Andy skated practices with the Thief River squirt team, in the old arena where the boys had skated, and struck up more friendships. We met with Duane Glass, at his warehouse. Duane gave Andy and Alex bags full of candy bars; the boys thought that was the greatest. We met with Fred Dablow, who hadn't changed much from high school days and who was a wealth of information; his mother had kept a scrapbook that was invaluable. Rod Collins drove over from North Dakota and spilled the beans about the blizzard; Jackie did not know about that blizzard experience until he read a rough draft of the screenplay. We went to Miss Skomedahl's farm just before Christmas and had lefse and cookies in her kitchen. She gave Andy a pocket watch that had belonged to her brother. We visited Paul, Caroline, and Charlie Bedard, wonderful people, and many other folks who were somehow involved with the team, the school or the radio station. We drove back to Minneapolis and interviewed many more people there including Jim Hall and Glen Carlson. I met with Oscar Mahle in Duluth, and Larry Johnson of Edina and Jerry Norman, owner of All Star Sports, New Hope. I had known all of these men when we attended the University of Minnesota. They were all on the Gopher team and in 1961 were third nationally in the NCAA playoffs in Denver. Of course, much was done on the phone, but our first trip set the tone of the project and the knowledge that we were very much supported in the endeavor.

Without Colleen I couldn't have written the book. We didn't have a computer at that time so everything was written on a typewriter on the dining room floor. Every change meant that the page and the following pages had to be retyped. Colleen was the organizer and the person always ready with suggestions. Both being English teachers we had great fun with words. We had a wonderful time during this period of creating. She kept a log of everyone we contacted and made lists of addresses and phone numbers. When we did get a computer Colleen transferred all her notes and the script onto it.

Without Glen Carlson I couldn't have written the book. All the "boys" had good memories but Glen had a penchant for details and his memory jarred the others. He is a meticulous person and didn't let even the smallest error go by. In the early days of the screenplay we were Fed-Exing the pages back and forth from Wilmette to Minneapolis. Glen has the rare ability to keep people pumped up and producing. Glen's secretary, Debby, was a great help to us also. Thanks, Debby.

My husband, Darrell, and my son, Andy, were behind me every step of the way, putting up with odd hours, a glorious (happy) mess in the dining room and lots of Taco Bell and Pizza Hut! They have also had to "hang out" while I've autographed and sold books at bookstores and hockey rinks.

The era after the writing of the script was exciting because the screenplay was hopping from one movie house to another. Colleen's log grew and grew.

With the passage of time I decided to turn the screenplay into a book. Ed MaGaa, author of *Native Wisdom*, published the first edition. I thank you Ed, for having the faith in the story to put your money behind it!

I would also like to thank Glenda Gausen for her help and support in whatever I have needed regarding the book.

The success of the sale of the book belongs to the following people to whom I owe a deep gratitude. Thank you so much to the following folks who made the book visible to the public: Charlie Bedard for unflagging enthusiasm and efforts in behalf of *River of Champions;* Virg Foss, Grand Forks Herald; Don Boxmeyer, Mike Fermoyle and Gregg Wong, St. Paul Pioneer Press; Kevin Pates, Duluth News-Tribune; Doug Johnson, Shane Frederick and Bob Utecht, Let's Play Hockey; John Gilbert, Doug Grow and Roman Augustoviz, Minneapolis Star-Tribune; Mike Nistler, St. Cloud Times; Sharon Raboin, Green Bay Press-Gazette; Tom Yelle, Anoka County Union; Marv Lundin, Thief River Falls Times; Steve Webb, Rochester Post-Bulletin; Paul Bergquist, Minnetonka Sun Current; Don Jorstad, KTRF; Rich Leonard, who travelled to Thief River Falls with his Pee Wee team and wrote about his experiences; Wally Shaver; Mike Woodley, KFAN; Steve Cannon, WCCO; Herb Brooks; and John Kuderle, of Bookman.

* * *

Now to answer some readers' questions. The number one question I have been asked concerning *River of Champions* is if the ice scenes were true. A resounding "yes!" The scenes are as meticulously accurate as memory could serve and each ice scene was documented by players on both teams whenever possible. Each injury is factual. Miss Skomedahl and her Shakespeare are true. J.C. and Rolle are true. The antecdotes on Jimmy and Cookie's strength are real events. The boys and coaches of the opposing teams are, in fact, as they were. The towns and cities are real places.

The second most asked question is, "What happened to the boys?" As with any group the answer is diversified. The following is a vignette on each:

Jimmy Reese made a fortune in Alaska.

Cookie is in Denver.

Jim Hall went on to play hockey at the University of Minnesota-Duluth for a year then transferred to Michigan State. He and two partners own a meat processing company in Kansas. He and Janice married and live in Kansas.

Rod works for a post office in North Dakota and augments that with construction during the summers.

Fred has worked for Tony Dorn, Inc. in Thief River Falls as a salesman for the past twenty years.

Art lives north of Thief River Falls. He owned a taxi company in Thief River Falls for years but gave that up and currently works for Artco.

Glen attended the University of North Dakota. He played for the rugged Thieves team for several years during that time. After graduation he went on to Texas A & M for his Masters degree and has had a career with the Minnesota Department of Transportation in traffic management: currently as manager of the Traffic Management Center in Minneapolis. Angie married Glen; they live in Fridley, Minnesota.

Duane owns a sports card shop in Thief River Falls after retiring from owning a beer distribution company in Thief River Falls.

Jackie went on to play for the Rochester Minnesota Mustangs (a Senior team in the USHL), then to the Mid-America league in Green Bay, Wisconsin. From that team he was selected to play for the prestigious USA National Team for 3 years. They played in Geneva, Colorado Springs (the team that won the Bronze) and the third was in Stockholm, Sweden. Jackie currently lives in Green Bay with his family.

Sadly, Chipper was killed in a car accident in Duluth, Minnesota in 1969.

* * *

The second printing of *River of Champions* is largely due to Colleen Wasner and David Starke, my editors. I thank them for getting the fires burning in me again to get the story back out there so more people can enjoy it. They spent hours carefully proofing the book and getting it ready for publication. This is not an easy job. It is tedious and time consuming and I appreciate all their efforts into preparing the book into as perfect a copy as possible. Thank you both.

A final thanks to the many people I don't know who come up to me to tell me how much they loved the story and to everyone, everywhere who has supported the book.

I appreciate you all.

December 1998

*please turn the page
for a preview of*

Henry Boucha:
Star of the North

by
Mary Halverson Schofield

Coming Soon!

1

for the love of henry

The screaming 15,000 fans in the brightly lit Met Center rose to their feet in one immense swell as the scrappy Warroad Warriors hockey team, from the tiny town so far north it almost touched Canada, skated onto the ice for the 1969 Minnesota State High School Championship. Their entrance sent a charge through the crowd like an invisible bolt of lightning, causing the fans to cheer, yell, whistle and clap in unbridled ecstasy. The ovation lasted two full minutes as the teenage boys, trying to act nonchalant but feeling numb knots in their stomachs, tried to absorb its meaning.

Warroad's Coach Roberts, knowing full well the meaning of this tribute, stood looking up emotionally at the tumultuous fans. He had hardly had time to reflect on these last few weeks and now surely wasn't the time, but he felt the sense of history being made. His team had worked miracles to get here and they deserved this rip-roaring homage.

Warroad's team was captained by #16, the already legendary seventeen year old American Indian boy, Henry Boucha. Henry had led this underdog team 'seat of their pants' style to this final game of the 1969 Minnesota State High School Championship.

Again, as he had many times over the years, Roberts asked himself how he could have been lucky enough to have coached this phenomenal kid, this poised and mystical figure, whom he was convinced was the finest hockey player to have ever come out of Minnesota.

One small section of the arena held the "green jackets," possibly a thousand strong: the rival Edina supporters from the wealthy suburban school, who had been labeled "cake eaters" by the less monied. The rest of the fans were cheering for the underdog team from little Warroad, the Cinderella team of the tournament.

Lanky Henry Boucha stepped onto the glimmering ice almost lazily. He skated slowly around the large frozen oval toying with a puck as the other skaters whizzed by him. He was six feet tall, awkward, and looked mostly arms and legs. His hockey breezers were too short, as was his ill-fitting jersey, and he looked out of place among the other skaters. Henry had an uncanny sense of peace about him as he stretched and shook out his shoulders. He didn't seem to notice the other players or, for that matter, the insane crowd that was cheering, for the most part, for him. Henry looked, for all the world, like a lollygagger: someone there to watch from the bench and possibly give the other skaters encouragement.

The crowd knew better. They quieted as the warm-ups started but kept their gaze on Henry because they knew that when the spirit moved him Henry would put on his show. He casually skated around the far end, coming from behind the net, and almost seemed to yawn as he started down ice. The crowd readied expectantly as they saw a patch of clear ice open up as the players ahead of him rounded the net on the other end. Henry twitched slightly and then, as if he had been ignited like a Roman Candle, his bulk streaked down the ice. The sight was electrifying and the delighted crowd exuded an admiring, prolonged "oooooohhhhhhhhhhhhhhh."

"Damnedest thing I've ever seen in my life," Glen Carlson, a former hockey all-stater from Thief River Falls, Minnesota, said to his friend, Mike Rabe. Mike nodded as he kept an intent eye on Henry.

Henry settled back into his slow and quiet routine as the crowd marveled and waited expectantly for another burst. They were not to be disappointed. Henry let his teammates get ahead of him again and then he took off bounding like a startled deer as he skimmed the ice. The crowd "ooooohhhhhhhhhhhhhhhed" again; this time he didn't pause in between sprints but kept it going like a double axle. "Swoosh," like a bat out of hell, he tore up the ice, thrilling the spectators again and this time they "ooooohhhhhhhhhhhhhhhed" even longer.

The current in the air held a silent whisper that told the fans beforehand that this game would thereafter be known as the Game-of-Games of any Minnesota State High School Tournament contest. The Minneapolis newspapers hailed it as a David and Goliath event. Could the team from the edges of the north with its superstar #16 beat the powerhouse team from the large and privileged school?

Cameras flashed and TVs strained to keep up with Henry. The media couldn't get enough of him. He was a sensation, "the rage," and everyone wanted a piece of his action.

The teams gathered for their introductions, which hushed the crowd in preparation of the announcements of the boys' names. The Edina team was introduced first to a few "yea, rah rah's" as each boy skated out to center ice as his name was called. The crowd had a 'let's get on with it' attitude as they waited, then the charge ignited again as the booming voice said, "And now for the Warroad Warriors!" As each Warrior shot out to center ice a rousing cheer went up from the stands. The announcer skipped #16 then, after the entire Warroad team had been announced, he took a deep breath and, like an ancient announcing the Roman Emperor he almost sang: "Hen-er-y Booooou-chaaaa!" Henry skated out low and long, dazzling the standing, screaming mob who did not let up their boisterous salute to him for ten minutes.

The fans envisioned this Indian boy from the north living in a teepee and eating wild rice when he wasn't amazing them on the ice. He was a pure hero of heroes who spoke to their heart. There was no doubt about it, the fans loved Henry Boucha.

River of Champions

may be ordered from

Snowshoe Press
P.O. Box 24334
Edina, MN 55424

Send $11.95 per book US / 14.95 Canada
(*Minnesota residents add .84 sales tax*)
plus $1.50 shipping (add .50 per additional book).
Check or Money Order only.
Please remit in US funds.

Number of Copies _____

Amount Enclosed $ _____

Name_____

Address_____

City_____

State_____   Zip_____

Phone Number _____-_____

Thank You